I HAVE GLORIA KIRBY

I HAVE GLORIA KIRBY

RICHARD HIMMEL

CUTTING EDGE

ISBN-13: 978-1-952138-16-4

Published by
Cutting Edge Publishing
PO Box 8212
Calabasas, CA 91372
www.cuttingedgebooks.com

CHAPTER ONE

It came back the minute I saw her again. Everything. All at once. The way it used to be. There was the crazy way my blood ran when she walked into a room; the hot spot under my collar when she was near me; the terrible tearing of my insides telling me how much I wanted her, wanted to have her; the skip beat of my heart and the dizzy, almost drunk feeling in my head. All these things were back again. Even the marvelous quiet that comes with the afterglow of love, the hours of being alone together in wordless talking—that feeling was back, too.

And it might have stayed, we might have picked up and gone on as though the years that had passed were nonexistent, if—if this had been night. If I had been seeing her again in the night light, this excitement might have stayed inside me, caught in my throat, rushing in my blood.

But it wasn't night. The light of the morning was bright and intense. It came through the windows of my office with the harsh clarity of a floodlight, and I could see clearly the years between the last time I had seen Gloria Kirby and now, that moment as she stood in the door.

Her hair had been brown then, drab in the winter but wonderfully highlighted by the summer sun. It was all a glare of highlights now, bleached to a brash blondeness. The careful layers of paint on her skin couldn't camouflage the lines around her eyes or the soft sags that had come to be around her mouth and under her chin.

Don't get the idea that this new Gloria Kirby wasn't something to look at. Her face had changed, become hardened and sadder. But probably to most guys she was more attractive than she had been. It's just that I carried a picture of her in my mind and it was different from what I was seeing.

She seemed empty, somehow. All that wonderful vitality and spirit seemed drained out of her, leaving a cold void of nothingness. Maybe no one but I could see how it was with her. Maybe nobody but I had known her so well.

Even in the beginning heat of the day she was huddled in a big mink coat, holding it tightly around her, her fingers clutching the soft fur.

I stood up slowly, not saying anything for a few minutes.

She didn't move from the doorway. Then she said my name, almost whispering it, testing the saying of it. "Johnny."

"Hello, Kitten."

"Johnny…" This time it was more than saying my name. It was saying a lot of things. "Johnny. Johnny." She ran to me and I could feel her body collapse as my arms went around her. She kept repeating my name over and over again until it wasn't my name any more but a kind of chant, a wailing.

"Easy, Kitten. Take it easy."

"Hold me tight, Johnny. Hold me tight."

I held her as tight as I could. She was shivering under all that fur and crying hard. Crying not with tears alone, but with her whole body, the dry kind of tears that are so hard to cry. There was a minute that I thought all of this was for me, that seeing me again was affecting her this way. But only for a minute. Gloria Kirby was scared. She was shaking with her fright.

Holding her away from me, I looked at her face. The tears had streaked her make-up. "Get hold of yourself, Kitten." I pressed her arms hard. "Come on, snap out of it."

She bit her lip and tightened her body. "I'm all right, Johnny. Really I am." She smiled then and backed away.

"It's just that I haven't seen you for such a long time."

"Something is wrong, baby. What is it?"

"No, really, Johnny. It's nothing, nothing at all. I—I had an early appointment this morning and I happened to remember that your office was close by and I—"

"You'd better sit down." I led her over to the couch.

"You wouldn't have a drink for a lady, would you, Johnny?"

"I think some breakfast might set better," I said. "Have you eaten yet?"

"Breakfast?" She laughed a little and threw her head back. It was there again for a moment in that gesture, the girl I had known, the girl I had loved. "Do you remember our flat on Fourteenth Street, Johnny? Do you? Twelve bucks a month we paid, out of what you made and I made. Every morning I fixed breakfast for you. Do you remember that? Except Sunday, and then you made breakfast for me and we ate in that crazy bed that pulled out of the wall. Do you remember, Johnny?" She gasped for breath. "Was it real or is it something I made up? Did it happen?"

"It was real, baby."

She fumbled in her purse for a cigarette, lit it with a shaking hand. "You want to know something, Johnny? I haven't made breakfast for anyone else since then. When we broke up—when I went away—God, it seems like a million years ago—I had my first taste of dough then, Johnny. I knew what it was to pick up a hotel phone and have them send breakfast upstairs. I thought what a sap I had been, sweating it out with you. Working for you, cooking and washing clothes. I told myself I'd never be a sap like that again for any man. Never." Her voice softened. "There have been a lot of men since then, Johnny, and I never made breakfast for any of them. No one since you." She took another deep breath and it became a rasping gasp for air. "I've missed it, Johnny. I've missed it terribly." I started toward her. The years had vanished again and things were the way they had been on Fourteenth

Street. But she stopped me. "Stay away, Johnny. Please. Get me a drink like a good boy, will you?"

I kept a bottle in my bottom drawer. I handed it to her and she took a stiff swallow and set it on the floor.

"Something is wrong. What is it?"

"Be smart, Johnny. Tell me to get the hell out of here. I'm trouble, you know that. I'm plenty of trouble. I've been trouble to any guy who has touched me. Except you.I don't want to be trouble for you. Tell me to get the hell out of here and get out of your life."

"If you're in hot water, Gloria—"

"Me in hot water?" She laughed, took another swallow out of the bottle. "That's a hot one. Look at me, Johnny. Look at this coat. You know how much it cost? You know how much this ring cost? Do you? You know how many more I got? Me in trouble? It couldn't happen to me, Johnny. Not to Gloria Kirby."

She wasn't fooling me any. There was something wrong and I couldn't figure it. It was a cinch she hadn't come to put a touch on me. Where Gloria Kirby walked, money walked right with her.

With effort and unsteadily, she got up from the couch. "Nice to see you, Johnny. Drop in and see me when you're in my neighborhood." She took one step and collapsed to the floor, a mound of beautiful woman and beautiful mink. Her purse had fallen, too, and the contents spilled on the floor.

I stood there, wide-eyed, not believing what I saw. Wads of dough, brand-new money in neat packages, were scattered all over the bare wooden floor. Not small stuff, either; these were packages of thousand-dollar bills.

She had come a long way, Gloria Kirby had, and she had come no way at all.

We had started in the same place, the same rough neighborhood, walking the same dirty streets looking for excitement, looking for answers. You had to be tough to survive in that

4

neighborhood, there was so little to be had and so many people trying to get it.

I don't remember any more how Gloria and I met. It's not important. We were alike in many ways. Both of us were part of the neighborhood, born in it and rooted to it. But there was something in each of us—call it having a star in your eye or a secret dimension, I don't know what it was, but it drew us together.

In the years before the war, I was on the fence between becoming a hoodlum and being a right guy. I was tough enough for the gang, tough enough to be a leader. But I was afraid to get mixed up with them; not afraid of getting hurt or landing in jail, but I was afraid that once I started I'd never stop, I'd want to be the top man, blind to everything but being the top man. I knew all the ropes. I knew dope peddling, blackmail, policy rackets, and all the other rottenness that breeds in big cities.I wanted what was at the top of all that, the money and the security and the being free from wanting.

There was another way to get it, too,—the right way, the storybook way. I was going to have to make up my mind which direction to take. The two directions gnawed at me constantly and I did nothing, not moving either way. It was at this time that Gloria Kirby and I moved into the apartment on Fourteenth Street.

Let's get this straight: Gloria was not a virgin flower when we first got together. I say this because what happened to her isn't really one man's fault. It's not my fault and it wasn't entirely Danny Nelson's fault. Danny was the guy she finally wound up with, as high as you could go in the strata of racketeers. Gloria was the way she was and she had been that way ever since she found out about the birds and the bees and what went on in the shed behind the church. I had always wondered why the caretaker never locked that shed, but I was glad he didn't, and Gloria was glad too.

We lived together for more than a year. It was good living, better in retrospect than it seemed at the time. Our lives were so simple then. As I looked at her lying on the floor of my office, it didn't seem possible that it was the same girl, the sandy-haired kid I had loved and had pillow fights with and danced with to tinny juke-box music and held hands with as we lay side by side on the wet grass in the park looking up at the stars.

It wasn't that we stopped loving each other. We never even talked about love. One morning at breakfast Gloria said, "Johnny, I'm leaving."

At the time, I didn't feel anything. This was a girl and I had had her and there would be others. "O.K.," I said.

"I've got a chance to go to California."

"O.K."

"Don't you want to know who with, Johnny?"

"Sure. Who with?"

"Mickey Dwyer," she said.

It was none of my business. I guess I didn't really care very much, I was so caught up in my own problems. It was taking a lot of energy and concentration to sit on the fence the way I was. The rackets were so easy, just reach out and touch them. But the other thing, being a lawyer, being what I thought a lawyer was, that held the real temptation and fascination for me. It was a birthday cake a kid dreams about and never gets.

I got off the fence finally. Maybe Gloria's leaving gave me the shove that was needed. I made it the hard way, being a lawyer. It was rough and tough, but I got what I wanted, the diploma on the wall. Dollar-wise, the boys in the rackets did better than I. Like Mickey Dwyer, the guy Gloria went to California with. Dwyer is right in there between being a high-class hoodlum and a first-class operator. But he does all right. He drives a Buick.

"I'm going to miss you, Johnny," she had said. "Mickey is all right, but it won't be like being with you. You know that."

"You're sure you want to go with Mickey? He likes things pretty exotic, you know."

She didn't say anything, so I figured I wasn't telling her anything she didn't know. She could take care of herself.

After she left, I moved out of the old neighborhood and lost track of her. When she began hitting the big time, her picture was in the paper once in a while or in a magazine. She was the queen of the gangsters' molls, she moved from continent to continent as easy as I cross a street. She wore the best clothes and lived in the best houses and stayed in the best hotels. She could have been in the movies but she didn't need that. She had everything money could buy.

She also had Danny Nelson, and Danny Nelson was the biggest and best in the underworld. Funny thing about Nelson, in a lot of ways he was a cute guy. He was part of the old neighborhood, a couple of years older than I. He had brains and cunning, an invaluable sense of timing. I always said that Nelson was a terrible waste of talent. With all the stuff he had on the ball, if he had channelized it in another direction he could have been President if he wanted. But he didn't want that. He wanted to control gambling and dope and prostitution and God knows what else.

We were born on the same street, me and Danny and Gloria. But we were in different leagues now; they were millions of dollars away from me. And yet Gloria lay at my feet, and where Gloria was, Danny wouldn't be far away.

Before I even bothered about her, I shoved the packages of money back in her purse. There was some other stuff, too: a compact and cigarette case, keys, and a needle, a regular hypo needle. There was a little dope left in it. So she had come to that, I thought. The excitement of living with Danny wasn't enough. She needed dope. I jammed it all back into the purse before I picked her up and stretched her out on the couch. I forced some liquor in her mouth and she came to for a minute, opened her eyes once, then closed them again. I rubbed her hands to get the circulation going.

It was while I was in this position that Tina walked into my office without knocking. Tina always walked into my office without knocking. She never expected to find anyone there. And she always walked in talking. This time was no exception.

"If you talk to me real nice, Counselor," she was saying, "and give me a big, wet kiss, I'll buy your lunch today." She stopped when she saw I wasn't at my desk. It didn't take her long to find me. "Pardon me, Mr. Maguire. I didn't realize you were busy."

"Don't be funny, Tina. She passed out."

Tina saw the bottle. "It must have been quite a party. Are *you* still sober?"

"I tell you she's fainted."

"Because you're so irresistible? I've felt that way when you're near me, Counselor, but somehow I always managed to pull myself together and stay on my feet."

"You've got a damn evil mind, that's what you have."

"With almost anyone else, I might believe the story, Johnny. But I know you so very well."

"Shut up and come over and help me."

Tina walked over to the couch, still not believing what I was telling her. "Oh, look at all the mink." She blew on Gloria's coat. "Aren't we getting dressy, Counselor? Aren't we ever."

"Put those books under her feet."

"I'm a public stenographer, Buster, not Florence Nightingale."

"This is no joke, Tina. For Christ's sake, help me here. She's really sick."

Then Tina realized I wasn't kidding. She moved fast then, pushed me away, and brought Gloria around quickly. The first thing Gloria whispered was "The needle. In my purse."

Tina looked back at me. I was already fumbling in Gloria's purse. "Get that coat off her and pull up her sleeves."

"What do you—"

"Stop yapping and do as I say."

Her arm was covered with the telltale needle marks. I gave her the injection, emptying out the syringe. Tina watched the whole performance wide-eyed. "I guess there are some things," she said, "that a girl doesn't learn at business college. Is that dope?"

"Yeah."

"Johnny, I'm sorry that I—"

"Never mind that. You'd better get out of here."

"All right, Johnny, but I really—"

"And pretend that you never came up here. You never saw anything. You never saw her and you never saw me this morning."

She was walking toward the door. "All right, Johnny. Whatever you say."

"And Tina?"

She hesitated without turning back to me. "Yes, Counselor?"

"Were you serious about buying lunch?"

"Sure."

"Then come here."

She came to me slowly, almost shyly, and I kissed her. "Was that big enough and wet enough?"

"Delightful, Counselor. You can even have pie à la mode for dessert."

"Now, beat it, baby. And remember you never saw any of this."

It took about ten minutes before Gloria got hold of herself enough so that she could talk. Then she said, "Let me get out of here. I don't want to get you mixed up in this."

"You came here for help. Tell me what it is."

"There was no one else to turn to. It had to be you, Johnny. I'm sorry you have to see me like this, but I had no place to go. There was no one else who would understand."

"Come on, spill it. Get it out of your system."

"Light me a cigarette, Johnny." I lit two, one for each of us.

"Like old times, isn't it, Johnny?" She took a deep drag.

"Never mind old times, Gloria, what have you done?"

She let out a waft of smoke. "I've double-crossed Danny Nelson."

"How? Another guy?"

"If it had been another guy, do you think I'd be worried? No, there have been other guys and Danny knows it. He doesn't like it, but he can't do anything about it. There's something that Danny loves more than me. Money. I've stolen money from him. Seventy thousand dollars. It's there in my purse."

"What for?"

She seemed calmer now and stronger. She stood up without trouble and walked over to the window. "That's a good question. What for? For a lot of reasons, Johnny. Because I can't stand it anymore. I can't stand the life I'm leading. I can't stand the tension every minute and the smoke and the dope and the men and all the rottenness. They're trying to get Danny. The government is. You know how? By getting me to talk. I could talk enough to send half the racketeers in this country to jail for life. I can't stand it anymore. I'm afraid to walk down a street. I'm afraid to—" She turned suddenly. "I'm going to get out of here, Johnny. I can't get you mixed up in this. The one decent thing left in my life is the years we had together." She grabbed her purse and started for the door.

I grabbed her arm and pulled her back. "I'm in it now, Gloria. You got me into it the minute you walked into this office. Now, tell me the story, all of it."

"Johnny, I don't want you in it. This is big. There's so much involved."

"Come on, baby, get it off your chest."

"I'm fed up with it, that's all. I can't take it anymore. I know too much, too damn much. The government guys keep pressuring me to talk. Danny and the other boys know it. They're scared to death that the government will get me on an investigation or something and I'll have to talk. My life wouldn't be worth two cents if Danny hadn't been smart. You know what he made me do? He made me write out everything I know, about all the boys and all the rackets and everyone who is involved." She laughed. "Everybody but Danny. I didn't write nothing about Danny. He made me write all this and put it in a vault. No one can get to it unless something happens to me, unless someone tries to kill me. That's the only way they won't dare to touch me."

"Except Danny," I said. "What you wrote doesn't say anything about him."

"Yes. Yes, no one will dare touch me except Danny. That's why I'm scared."

"What about the dough?"

"You're going to think I've gone soft in the head. But I thought there was only one way out and that was to have enough dough to get away, to get somewhere to breathe fresh air. I don't want to skip the country or anything like that. I thought maybe I'd dye my hair and change my appearance and find a place to live in a small town or someplace where it's quiet. I never lived in a small town, Johnny. I've never known what it's like just to sit somewhere where there isn't smoke and noise. You think I'm nuts, don't you? You think Gloria Kirby is the last one in the whole world to live in a cottage somewhere and take care of the garden. Nuts or not, that's what I want to do."

"And that's where the dough comes in?"

"Yes. Danny don't give me much at a time. There's always one of his boys trailing after me when Danny isn't there. They carry the money. I couldn't hock enough from the stuff I got to last me for a long time. I needed enough so that I wouldn't ever have to go back anywhere where they might know me."

"Did you try asking Danny for it?"

"He laughed when I told him what I wanted to do. You didn't laugh, did you, Johnny? I told Danny what I wanted. I told him about a little house somewhere, near a lake maybe. He laughed at me. He didn't believe me. I tried to tell him how bad I wanted it, how fed up I was with everything, how I didn't think I could breathe no more if I had to stay in the city with him. You know what he thought? He thought there was another guy and I wanted him to set this thing up for another guy. He called me every rotten name in the book. They hurt, Johnny. For the first time they hurt. Because they're true, maybe. Because I am all those rotten things. But I don't want to be like that no more. You can understand that, can't you? I don't want to be those things. I just want to be nobody living in a little house in the country."

"I guess I can understand some of it better than Danny. I knew you before he did."

"Danny says I could never do it. He got me started on dope. He did it purposely, I think. He's got the dope market sewed up all over the country. Danny got me on dope because he knew that way I could never get away from him. He thought once I got the habit I'd keep coming back for it, and if you take dope, no matter where you are, Danny Nelson can find out about it."

"You think you can get cured?"

"I know I can, Johnny. If I could get away I could cure myself. It don't make no difference what doctors say. If I could get away in the country, by myself, I could stop, taper off. It would be easy. I know I could do it."

"So you stole the money?"

She laughed. "Everybody steals from everybody, don't they, Johnny?" She held her purse upside down and everything spilled to the floor again. "Look at it. Isn't it pretty? So clean and new."

"Are you out of your head? Put it back. What if someone came in here and saw it?"

"It's so pretty, Johnny. So clean and new. I could get a new start with it."

I picked up the stuff and put it back in her purse. "How did you get it?"

"I waited until I knew there was going to be a job pulled. Whenever a job is pulled anywhere in the country, the dough comes to Danny. He likes to hold it and look at it. He's got a place to hide it in the apartment until he's ready to put it in the vault. It happened last night. They brought the dough and I watched Danny holding it and looking at it. Then this morning, before he got up, before I came here, I took it. I took it and I ran." She seemed to realize what she had done then, and it made her cold. She pulled the coat together and thrust her hands deep into the pockets. "Then I got scared. Then I realized just what I was doing. I realized the way Danny loves that money, the way he loves to hold it. I knew then I'd never get away with it, he'd get me no matter where I went or what I did. I'm a dumb dame, Johnny. I got crazy ideas, I want crazy things. I should have known Danny wouldn't let me get away with it. I should have known Danny would never stop until he got me for double-crossing him. Nobody ever gets away with double-crossing Danny. He'll kill me, Johnny. He'll kill me." She lowered her head and began to cry again.

"How long ago did this happen?"

"I don't know. This morning. Just before I came here. I started to go to the Union Station. I was going to take a train somewhere. Then I got cold feet and came here." She ran to me. "Help me, Johnny. Get me away. I can't stand it anymore. I've got to get away."

I looked at my watch. She had been in my office about twenty-five minutes. Altogether she had probably been gone from Danny's apartment about an hour. "Danny was still sleeping when you left?"

"Help me, Johnny, help me."

I pulled her to her feet and shook her until she could look at me and stop crying. "Was Danny still sleeping when you left the apartment?"

"Yes."

"How long does he usually sleep?"

"I don't know. It depends. Late, sometimes."

"You've got to get this money back before he misses it."

"Don't make me go back there, Johnny. Don't make me. Please, don't make me go back there. I want to find a place in the country. Remember when you used to rent a car and we'd drive out and have a picnic in the woods? I want to go someplace like that, like the place we used to go on picnics. I always made you tuna-fish salad sandwiches. You still like tuna-fish sandwiches, Johnny? We could go together. There's plenty of dough for both of us."

"You've got to get the money back if there's a chance. It's the only way."

"He'll kill me, Johnny. Even if I bring it back he'll kill me. You don't know him like I do, you don't know what money means to him."

"Listen to me, Gloria. You haven't got a prayer of getting away with this. Me and the United States Army and Navy couldn't keep Danny from finding you, no matter where you went or what you did to change the way you look. If you want to get away, that's one thing. You can break it off with him and go where you want, but not with his dough. We can talk about that later. Right now you've got to get that money back before he misses it, do you understand?"

"But how, Johnny?"

"I'm not sure." I thought for a minute. "What's his phone number?"

"What for?"

"Never mind what for. Give me his number."

"Parkside 2-6947."

I dialed the number. "Keep quiet now," I told Gloria. A man's voice answered. "Danny?"

"Naw, this ain't Danny. You want to talk to Danny?"

"Can I? I didn't know if he was out of bed yet."

"Yeah, he's up." I heard some yelling going on in the room, but I couldn't make out any of the words. The man at the other end said, "You'd better call back later. I don't think Danny can talk on the phone right now."

I hung up quickly. It was too late. The excitement at the other end of the line could mean only one thing. Gloria Kirby was as good as dead unless I could think up something.

"Danny knows, doesn't he, Johnny?"

I nodded. Gloria didn't say anything. Her eyes were wide and glassy. She was reading the same handwriting on the wall. I was being a sap, I knew it then. I was putting my head in the noose right with Gloria. Sooner or later Nelson would find out that I was mixed up in it. The smart thing to have done was to call back Nelson and say that Gloria Kirby and the dough were sitting in my office, come and get them. That way, I would have been off the hook. Nelson would have even been indebted to me.

But I couldn't do that. It would be like putting a bullet through her myself. And I couldn't let her out on the street to be slaughtered. Maybe it had something to do with the fact that once I had loved her. I kept telling myself that even if that had never been, if she were a stranger, I still wouldn't do it, I still wouldn't let her walk out to her death without making an attempt to help her.

But I couldn't think of anything. All I knew was that she had to be hidden away. She had to be locked in a room some place and kept there until I had a chance to think and work out a plan. I called Tina at her office downstairs. The girl who works for her answered the phone.

"Phyllis, let me talk to Tina."

"Is this Johnny?"

I didn't want her to get suspicious, so I gave her the usual line. "This is Counselor Maguire."

"Well, Counselor Maguire, Miss Weston is taking dictation from Counselor Somebody Else and she can't come to the phone."

"Tell her it's important, Phyllis."

"I'll see if she will."

Tina came to the phone. "What's the matter, Johnny?"

"Who are you tied up with?"

"Jerry Miller."

"Can you shake him?"

"I suppose. What's the matter?"

"I need help and I need it fast."

"Did your girlfriend pass out again?"

"Let's cut the comedy, Tina. This is serious. Will you help?"

"Sure, Johnny. What do you want me to do? Wait a minute."
I heard her talk across the room. "Jerry, can this wait until later?
Something important has come up. Can you come back this
afternoon?" I heard him answering but couldn't distinguish the
words. Tina said, "Thanks a lot, Jerry. I'll do something special
for you someday to make up for it." There was a pause. "I can't
tonight. Honestly. I've got a date. Thanks, Jerry. I'll see you later."
Then back to me. "Johnny? O.K., go ahead."

"Why don't you give the guy a break, Tina? He's building up
a good practice."

"I've got a date tonight. With you, if you remember."

I had forgotten. There was a dance that night at one of the
country clubs put on by a local political group. I went every year
and hated it. The last year or two I had been taking Tina. She
thought the dances were swell. "Listen, Tina, I'm not sure I'm
going to be able to go tonight."

"No, you don't, Maguire. Dead or alive, you're going. I bought
a new dress for this clambake and I've spent three weeks getting
rid of dishpan hands and housemaid's knee so that I'll look rav-
ishing tonight. Dead or alive, you're going."

"We'll talk about it later. Right now I want you to go out and
do some errands for me. Write this down. Buy a small suitcase,
an overnight bag. It doesn't have to be expensive. Maybe the
drugstore will have one of those canvas ones. And buy a tooth-
brush and tooth paste and whatever else a girl needs. You know
the kind of stuff I mean."

"Most girls need a man and most men don't fit into a suitcase."

"Very funny. What do you know about hair dyes?"

"Not a thing. My hair might be dull and mousy but it's the way God gave it to me, unlike certain ladies I have seen this morning."

"There must be something we can use to do a fast dye job, something black."

"There's a home dye thing they advertise on television. I'll see if I can get that. You want black?"

"Yes. And have you got a coat you can bring up?"

"I guess so. What happened to the mink?"

"Listen to me carefully. After you buy all this stuff, go back to your own office. Wait five minutes and then bring it up. Don't use the elevator. Use the back stairs."

"It's five flights!"

"It'll do you good. You're getting fat. You're getting a ring around your middle."

"John Maguire! Of all the colossal—"

"Some other time we'll talk about your middle. Right now you've got to move fast. Get going." Tina hung up before I finished the sentence.

I turned back to Gloria. She seemed to have relaxed. She lay on the couch looking up at the ceiling. "You all right, baby?"

"Funny," she said, "you wonder about people who know they're going to die, you wonder what they think about."

"Nothing is going to happen to you."

She didn't even hear me. "Like you see in the movies, guys going to the chair, and you wonder what they think about while they're waiting. Do you want to know what I'm thinking about, Johnny? Do you?"

"Sure, kid. What is it?"

"I'm thinking about us, the way we used to be. How long ago was it, Johnny? Ten years? That's not so long, is it? I was twenty. I suppose compared to most girls I knew a lot for being only twenty. I'd been through a lot. I'd give up all the dough in my purse to be back there again, with you in that little apartment. I wouldn't care. If I had it to do over again, it would all be different, I'd do it different. I'd stay with you, Johnny. I would stay with you and make you happy."

"Don't talk like that, Gloria. Nothing is going to happen to you."

"You don't believe that, Johnny. You know Danny is going to get me." She got up suddenly and came over to the desk. "When a person is going to die they get a last request, don't they?"

"Sure, I guess they do."

"You know what mine would be? I'd want to go on a picnic like we used to do." She looked out the window. "It's a wonderful day for a picnic, Johnny. We could go out in the woods and run and laugh just like we used to do. Then when it starts to get dark we could—we could make love. It's wonderful to make love in the woods. We could pretend that nothing has happened, that it's ten years ago, that it's—I could pretend," she said. "Maybe it wouldn't even be pretending." She looked straight at me. "What about you? Could you pretend?"

I couldn't look at her. A guy can be only so tough. I didn't say anything. Gloria laughed softly. "I'm sorry, Johnny. You're doing enough for me. I guess I can't expect you to love me again." She went back and lay on the couch. Neither of us spoke until Tina came back. We were both thinking about the same things, the way things used to be with us. Remembering good times can create a mood, and I was near to being caught in that mood. It would have been so easy to go to the couch and lie beside her and say the things that she wanted to hear. It would have been so easy. And it would have been so dangerous.

Tina burst into the office in her usual style. "I've had a long talk with myself, Counselor, and I have decided that not only are you going to reimburse me for the fortune I spent in the drugstore, but you are also going to pay for the time I've lost from gainful employment. A girl has to eat, you know."

"Did you get everything?"

"Everything including aspirin in case your girlfriend gets a headache." She saw that Gloria was looking at her. "Well, look who's awake."

"Gloria, this is Tina Weston." Gloria didn't smile or say anything. I'm not sure that she even knew that Tina and I were in the room. She seemed to be in a trance.

We worked as fast as we could. The hair dye took quickly. Gloria had hair as black as jet. We scrubbed the make-up off her face and there was a great transformation. "You see," Tina said, "beauty isn't even skin deep. It's all on the surface."

The funny thing was that Gloria looked more like her old self this way, closer to the girl she had been.

"Gloria, listen to me. Listen carefully."

She didn't respond. I shook her a little. "Are you listening now? This is important."

"Yes, Johnny."

"I'm going to leave the office first. Wait about ten minutes. Do you have a watch?"

"No, I left it home."

"Well, try to figure out when ten minutes are up. Go downstairs and take a taxi to the Stevens Hotel. Takethis suitcase with you. Register at the hotel under the name of Marion Talbot. Have you got that?"

"Marion Talbot." She repeated the name. "Yes. I'll remember that."

"Somehow," Tina said, "she doesn't look like a Marion to me. What about Gertrude? Gertrude Talbot. I have a maiden aunt named Gertrude. I think the name would suit your—"

"Shut up!" I said. "Your name is Marion Talbot and you're from New York. Give them an address. Any address. Some number on Hudson Street. That's good enough. Any number on Hudson. Is that all right?"

"Yes."

"I'll be in the lobby of the hotel, but if you see me, pretend you don't know me. I'll hear what room you're in and then I'll come up there."

Tina said, "That'll be chummy. I may be in that lobby myself."

"You're going to get out of here and get out of here right now, Tina."

"After all I've done, you're going to push me out?"

"Please, Tina. Please. I'll see you later. I'll be back for lunch and I'll tell you all about it. I promise. Just keep your mouth shut until then. You don't know anything about anything. Now, please go, will you?"

"I'll go, but I don't like this. Any of it."

I pointed to the mink coat. "And get rid of that."

"What do you mean, get rid of it?"

"Get rid of it. Destroy it. It can't be found anywhere around here. Burn it if necessary."

Tina's eyebrows went up. "Bum a mink coat? Are you crazy, Johnny? The Business College Alumni Association excommunicates stenographers who burn mink coats. I wouldn't do it. A thing like that could change a girl's whole life."

"Tina," I said, "listen to me. Lives are at stake in this thing. I'm serious. That coat must be destroyed."

"Johnny, you aren't biting off more than you can chew, are you? Is she worth it?"

"Trust me, Tina, will you?"

"I wouldn't want you to get killed or anything, Johnny. You're irritating alive, but I'd kind of miss having you around."

"If you do as I say, everything is going to be all right. Now, please get going."

Gloria sat up. "If she wants the mink coat, Johnny, let her have it."

"We can't take a chance, Gloria, of Danny's ever finding any evidence that you've been here."

I HAVE GLORIA KIRBY

Gloria started to say something but Tina cut in. "Look, sister, I don't know who you are or why Johnny is doing this for you. It's his business. But when it comes to mink coats, I'm going to get my own in my own way." She turned to me. "The engineer is going to think I'm nuts when I throw this in the boiler."

"Disguise it some way. Wrap it in old legal briefs. You can figure out a way."

"O.K., Counselor, just keep your nose clean, will you? And your neck in one piece? For me, Johnny."

"I'll see you at lunch."

As soon as Tina left, Gloria said, "Is that your girl, Johnny? She's pretty."

"Never mind that now. You know what you're going to do. You're Marion Talbot, remember that. I'll get up to your room as quick as I can. I'll knock three times, fast. Don't let anyone else in. O.K?"

"What about the money?"

"I forgot about that. You better not take a chance carrying that around." I took it out of the purse and stuffed it under the seats of the couch. "I'll worry about it later. Now I'm going to take off. Wait until you think ten minutes has gone by. Then leave."

"All right, Johnny."

I got my hat and started for the door. "Good luck, Gloria." She didn't hear me. She had taken the mirror from her purse and was looking at her raw, tired face and her new drab, black hair, still damp. One hand was rubbing the surface of the plain cloth coat Tina had brought to her. I remember thinking again that Gloria had come a long way and she had come no way at all.

CHAPTER TWO

The Stevens is a damn big hotel. It was right out in the open, in the middle of everything and easy to find, so I figured that it would be a while before Danny got around to looking there. I never thought of it as any more than a stopgap measure, a temporary hideout until I had a chance to figure something out.

It went off like clockwork. It wasn't Gloria Kirby who walked in that lobby, it was a bent, beaten woman; the glamour had been scrubbed off and dyed black. I listened for the room clerk to call out her room number to the bellhop. It was 1702. I waited a few minutes longer than I thought necessary before going up.

I rapped at the door with three short knocks. Gloria opened it right away. "You all right, Gloria?"

"Sure. I'm all right."

"You did good, baby. Not even your own mother would have known it was you."

She looked into the mirror over the dresser. "You're wrong. She would have known. I look like her now. This is the way she looked, plain like this, and haggard from working all the time, taking care of all the kids."

"Listen, I want you to be careful here. Don't go out of this room for any reason. As soon as I leave go to bed and stay there. Have them send all your food up. For no reason leave this room. And if the telephone rings, it's going to be me, but just in case it isn't, disguise your voice. O.K.?"

She was so vague I couldn't be sure that she had heard anything I said. I went up to her. "You sure you understand, Gloria?"

"Understand?" When she saw my face next to hers in the mirror, she walked to the windows and stood there looking out over Lake Michigan. "I understand a lot of things, Johnny." Suddenly she opened both the windows, as high as they could go.

I ran to her. "What are you doing? What's the idea?"

"Don't be frightened, Johnny. You think I'd jump down there?" She shook her head. "I wouldn't have the guts. No, I wouldn't. I only wanted the fresh air to come in. Smell it, Johnny. Smell the way the air is when it comes off the lake. What does it remind you of?"

It reminded me of a lot of things. It reminded me of her. She wasn't so different now. Ten years older, maybe, but stripped of the paint and stripped of the glitter, she wasn't so very different. Her coat was off and the wind caught her dress, pressing it against her body, outlining the wonderful contours of it. I could tell she had nothing on under it. Her body was the same and my eyes knew the sight of it and my hands knew the touching of it. All of that was hard to forget. When she was a thousand miles away I could remember it suddenly. And here in this room with her, there was no forgetting it; my mind wouldn't let me and the sweat on my hands wouldn't let me and that gnawing pull at the base of my stomach wouldn't let me forget it.

The smell of the wind blowing off the lake reminded me of many things. It reminded me that ten years ago I had been a sap to let her walk out of my life, that I had had the real thing and never known it but just accepted it, taken it as a matter of fact.

"What does it remind me of?" I asked. "I don't know, I suppose a lot of things."

She wheeled around. "Johnny," she began, and then she couldn't say anymore.

"All right, I'll say it, Kitten. It reminds me of everything—of the picnics and of the park and of the time we spent the week end at the sand dunes. It reminds me of everything it's reminding you of. Is that what you want me to say?"

"Yes." She said it simply.

"So where do we go from here?"

She looked down at the street seventeen floors below. "It's a long way down there," she said, and then she said, "I love you, Johnny. I've always loved you. I didn't know it for a long time. I didn't know it until I had everything in the world and there was still something missing. I knew it then because what I was missing was you." She moved close to me, the tightness of her body touched me. The points of contacts between us, the tips of her breasts, her hand on my arm, her legs against mine, all these things were electrically charged.

It went through my head all of it, all the things she had been since she left me, the men she had slept with, the dope and the liquor, all the degradation her wonderful body had been submitted to. But it didn't matter. I had to have her. I needed to have her with a hunger that the blood has, a powerful, surging kind of hunger building up inside me like the pressure in a compressor, physically needing to burst out, no outside power strong enough to hold it back.

I grabbed her roughly and through my mouth let out a spurt of this power, and the power was mixed with anger, and the softness of her mouth against my mouth was mixed with the hungry hardness of teeth. Our tongues were swords fencing each other.

It was a long kiss. It was a kiss saved up for ten years and it said what there was to say between us, the anger we had for each other and the anger we had for ourselves. It said the love there was between us at that moment and the wanting there was at that moment. When the kiss was over, we stood apart, breathing heavily, looking at each other, like boxers in the ring the second after the bell and two seconds before they return to their corners.

With one angry gesture she tore her dress from her body and she was naked beneath it. She was something to see, perfect. Nothing had changed the perfection of her, not the ten years and not the countless men who had had her. I just looked at her. There was nothing beyond her, nothing beyond the having of her. She could have been death, and knowing it, I would still have had to have her.

She kicked off her shoes and walked over to me. The color had come back to her face, natural color this time, and there was a faint smile on her lips. Her hands were steady as she loosened my tie. I stood there rooted to that floor as if I were stone as she began to undress me. She did it slowly, her hand lingering as she touched me, and each time she touched me a new excitement zigzagged through my body, each touch more exhilarating than the last. I didn't move, for I knew that once I moved a muscle nothing could stop me, and I wanted this to last, I didn't want it to be over quickly.

My clothes lay crumpled around me. She was kneeling at my feet unlacing my shoes, taking almost sensuous pleasure in the movement of her hands. When the shoes were untied she looked up at me from the floor. Her shoulders touched my knees and her hands made a straight line up my legs to my chest as she started to rise from the floor.

I could stand no more; the pressure was dangerously nearing its highest peak. I fell down beside her, clutching her, the weight of my body pinning her to the floor. She screamed. It was a scream that had to be screamed. Silently I was screaming it, too.

The sun was warmer as it reached its noonday peak. The wind from the lake had died down and no air seemed to be coming through the open windows. We hadn't said anything yet, either of us. Then Gloria said, "We're lucky, Johnny. You know why?"

"I know why," I said.

"We turned back the clock, didn't we? They say you can't turn back the clock, but we did. Just once. Just for such a little while."

I didn't say anything.

"You know, Johnny, we can't do it again. From now on we're what we are, not what we used to be. It'll never be the same again. I don't care, though. It's such a wonderful way to end it. I never thought it could have happened this way to me again, I never thought I could feel this way again."

"You're a funny girl, Kitten. You can be like this and you make it hard for me to believe that you can be the other way, the way you are with Danny Nelson, the way you are when they put your picture in the paper. Tough. Hard."

"No one knows me like this but you. And you'll never know me like this again. I'll never be like this again."

She was right, there was no use sweet-talking it. I knew it without knowing how I knew it. Once we got up from the floor she would be the gangster's moll again, her hand would shake from dope and from fright. She would be brittle and hard again.

A lot would happen once we got up from the floor. I'd have to figure a way to get her out of danger, to keep Danny Nelson off her track and off my track. And I remembered there was seventy thousand dollars under the cushions of the couch in my office. And Tina was going to buy my lunch.

Gloria stood up before I did. She put Tina's old coat over her nakedness. Then I got dressed. We didn't say anything to each other until I was ready to leave. "You remember what I said about not leaving the room and about answering the phone?"

"Yes, Johnny."

"Have you got any more stuff left in that needle?"

She shook her head.

"Are you going to need it? How are you going to get along without it?"

"I won't need it."

"Are you sure you'll be all right and won't do anything nuts?"

"I'll be all right."

I walked over to kiss her but she turned her face away from me. I understood that. She didn't want to spoil anything. "I'll get you out of this," I said.

"You're a sap, Johnny."

I knew what she was trying to do. I let it pass. "Good-by, Kitten," I said.

"Didn't you hear what I said? I said you were a sap." Her voice was hard now. Tough. Her lips were tight and her eyes were narrow. "You're a push-over for a few tears, Maguire. A slob like Danny says you are, a sentimental slob. What a sap I'm making out of you! You don't love me, Maguire. You love something that died ten years ago."

I kept my voice low and soft. "I know what I am," I said, "and I know what I feel. If I want to be a sap, that's my business."

"You think it meant anything just now, going to bed with you?" She shook her head angrily. "Not a thing, not a goddamn thing. I was playing you for a sap, that's all. Are you too much of a jerk to see that? Do you think I meant what I said about loving you? Never. You were always a punk and you'll always be a punk."

She couldn't have played the thing better if she had been born an actress. I let her talk. I let her get it out.

"Why do you think I came to you? Because you're so strong and so smart and no one else could help me? Not on your life. I came to you because no one else would be stupid enough to help me. No one else would be that much of a slob and a sap. Listen to what I'm calling you. Sap. *Sap.*" She kept saying the word until it reached near hysteria. I opened up my hand and let her have one full across the face.

It did the trick. She stopped talking for a minute and fell against me, sobbing softly. Then she said, "I love you too much to let anything happen to you, Johnny. I'm not worth it. Be smart, darling. Please, for once, don't be a sap. Take the dough and give it back to Danny. Tell him where to find me. I'll understand why you're doing it. Danny will be grateful to you. He may even cut you in for a couple of grand. Go on, Johnny, tell Danny where to find me."

"If you don't stop behaving like this, I might. Now, come on, Kitten, get hold of yourself. We've both got to be on our toes every minute if we're going to get away with this."

She hadn't even heard me. "When you tell Danny where to find me tell him I only got one request. Tell him when he comes to get me, tell him to do it when I'm sleeping so I won't know what's happening. I'm going to be dreaming about the house in the country. That's the way I want to die, dreaming about the house in the country. Tell Danny, please. Tell him that's the way I want to die. Tell him to do it for me that way please because he loved me once. Tell him that, will you, Johnny? Promise you'll tell him that."

"I'm going to lock the door and take the key. Get hold of yourself, Gloria, and don't forget what I told you to do."

"You won't be smart, will you, and do what I tell you?"

"A guy is built one way, Kitten. He can't change."

She walked away and looked out the open window again. "I guess what you say is right. You'll never change and Danny will never change. Neither will I."

We had said everything that needed saying and it was time for action. I locked the door, went downstairs, and took a cab back to my office.

CHAPTER THREE

Tina's sixth sense kept her from asking me anything about Gloria and what had happened at the hotel. She knew that part of me was miles away and she was smart enough not to try to bridge that distance. She realized that whatever was involved with Gloria Kirby was big-time stuff, so instead of talking about it she made chitchat over a sandwich, and it was easy to listen to or not listen to. Only one ear heard what she was saying. The other ear was listening to what my mind was saying about Gloria Kirby.

I wasn't in love with Gloria Kirby. I had never really carried a torch for her, but there had been times during periods of loneliness when I remembered how much I had loved her, and how bad I had wanted that love back. That wouldn't be happening any more. I had loved her again and the physical sensation of that love was everything I remembered it to be. Now it was over and it would never come back. And, strangely enough, I didn't want it to come back.

I realized that I was nuts to become so deeply involved with a girl who no longer had meaning to me, involved deeply enough to put my life in danger. I never underestimated Danny Nelson, not for a minute. But Gloria had come to me because she had no place to turn. I couldn't let her down. It wasn't for love, I wasn't doing this for love. For old times' sake? Maybe. Because I'm a goddamn sentimental Irisher with too much heart and no brains? That could be, too, I was thinking. But it didn't make any difference what I thought; I was in it now. I knew where Gloria Kirby was and I had seventy thousand bucks tucked under my sofa.

"You want pie à la mode, Counselor?"

"No, skip it. I'll take a rain check."

"She must be quite a doll to make you lose your appetite."

"Yeah," I said, "quite a doll."

"Feel like talking?"

I shook my head.

"I don't know what it's all about, Johnny, and I suppose it's none of my business, but—well, in a way it is my business. When somebody feels…" She lowered her head and looked a little coy. Tina is a big girl, good-looking and strong-looking. I forget sometimes that inside she's built like a little girl of five feet two with eyes of blue. Coyness in her always surprises me. "You know how I feel, Johnny," she went on. "In a way it entitles me to worry about you, want to take care of you. I mean, I think I have some rights even though you don't feel exactly the same way toward…" She looked up at me. There was a veneer of tears over her eyes. "You *do* feel that way about me, really, but you're too much of a lug to admit it."

"Christ, let's not talk about it now."

"All right, Johnny." She pushed back her chair, started to get up.

"Wait a minute, Tina," I grabbed her hand and she sat down again. "Don't ask me any questions about this, please. It's bad enough that I'm up to my neck in it. I don't want you involved, too. Just trust me."

"Trust you?" She threw back her head to stop the tears, to make them run back in her eyes. Successful businesswomen aren't supposed to cry. When she looked at me again she was all right. "Counselor, I would trust you with my life, with my money, with anything I've got. But when there's a woman involved, hell, no." She shook her head. "Never."

I changed the subject. "Do you know if there was anyone around here looking for me?"

"Not as far as I know."

"Any calls?" Tina ran a telephone service as well as a steno-graphic service. When I didn't answer my phone, it automatically rang down at her office.

"Mrs. Pincus called. Something about a divorce. She's not going through with it. She said to tell you Mr. Pincus came home."

"That son-of-a-bitch. Just when I thought I was going to make a little dough on his infidelity."

"You're so hardhearted, Counselor, standing in the way of true love just so you can turn a couple of fast bucks."

"It won't last. Even at sixty Mr. Pincus has that philandering look in his eyes. The next jane that walks by and looks at him twice, he'll take off after her again. I know the type."

Tina smiled. "So do I, but I love you anyway."

"You'd better beat it, baby. I've got some thinking to do."

"And I have work to do." She stood up. "What time will you pick me up?"

"Huh?"

"The dance at the country club, remember?"

"I keep forgetting. I'm not sure that—"

"Oh, yes, you are. You're not standing me up tonight. I bought a new dress without a top. Doesn't that tempt you?" I smiled at her. "All right," she said, "but at least let me get out so some of the other fellows can get a look or two."

"I'll see you later, Tina. And don't forget the check."

She picked the check up. "If I ever get a husband, he's going to seem so wonderful compared to you, Maguire." She smiled, stuck out her tongue, and took off.

Even after two more cups of coffee, I didn't have any answers. Gloria Kirby was in the hotel and I didn't know how to get her out of there or where to take her. I decided that maybe the next move wasn't my move, maybe Danny Nelson would make it. Sooner or later Danny Nelson would catch up to me, I knew that. He'd remember that once upon a time Gloria and I had been hooked up together, he'd give me the routine checkup. Nelson was the kind of operator who left no stone unturned.

I bought a newspaper at the stand and started to read it going up in the elevator. I thought maybe I would find some story about a robbery or something. Gloria had said that Nelson's boys had pulled a job to get this seventy grand. I was curious to see where it had come from. The paper didn't carry a line about any robbery involving that much cash.

Before going into my office, I stopped at Manny Green's office, three doors down the hall.

"What are you doing, Manny?"

Manny squeaked back in his swivel chair and hooked his thumbs under his suspenders. "I'm glad you asked me that, Johnny. I'm preparing a brief for a very important client. It's a big corporation. Millions of dollars are involved and they're counting on Manny Green to pull them through. Every lawyer in town was begging for the job. But they wouldn't have nobody but Manny Green."

"Best man in town," I said.

"I've been studying this case, checking and cross-checking references." He held up the Daily Racing Form. "It's a very difficult thing to decide. I think the only way I can win this case is if the track is muddy."

"How are you doing with the horses?"

"Not good, Johnny. Not good. On paper, I'm foolproof. I dope everything perfect. A beautiful, logical job of picking the winner. Except they don't win."

"Feel lucky?"

"Three across with kisses?"

"Get the cards."

"You want to play here?"

"No, we'd better play in my office. I'm expecting company."

"Enough for a poker game?"

"Maybe enough, but I don't think they'll be in the mood."

We went back to my office and started playing gin rummy. I like to play cards with Manny. He suffers. Every card he pulls is an effort, and he lays it on the pack with fear, certain that it's going to gin me.

"Manny?"

"Just a minute, Johnny." He put his finger to his mouth. "You took the nine of clubs but you didn't take the nine of diamonds. And you didn't take the ten of clubs. I don't understand it. You sure you're not playing some other game, you sure you're playing gin?"

"Look at the score." I was winning.

"He takes the nine of clubs but he doesn't take the nine of diamonds. So I throw the nine of hearts."

I picked it up. "Gin."

He threw down his cards. "I should never play cards with an Irishman. Never. So if you had a club run, why didn't you take the ten of clubs?"

"Count your cards, Manny. How many points?"

"Twenty-eight and gin makes fifty-three. Oh, my God, I'm on a blitz on the last game."

"Manny?"

"What?"

"Your wife is from out of town, isn't she?"

"Yeah. Peoria. It's one of the garden spots of the United States of America. It should get lost. Also my mother-in-law."

"They have a farm or something, don't they? Isn't that the place you send your kids in the summer?"

"Yeah. It's not much of a farm. It's a big house where my mother-in-law sits and writes letters telling my wife how we should live and how I shouldn't play the horses and how come I'm not rich like her nephew Sheldon, who is also a lawyer."

"They don't take any paying guests there, do they? I mean if someone wanted to get out of town for a couple of days, get away from everything?"

"You in trouble, Johnny?"

"Who, me? What kind of trouble would I get into?"

"I thought maybe you'd knocked up somebody or something, wanted to get out of town until it all blew over."

"No, this is a friend. I'm looking for a place to hide him."

"Better he should go to jail than spend three days with my mother-in-law. She'll not only find what he's hiding from, also she'll broadcast it all over Peoria and to her sister-in-law in Glencoe."

"Forget I mentioned it, will you?"

"I forgot already. Also I got a lousy hand."

We played until close to four o'clock, when the game was interrupted by the entrance of Danny Nelson and company.

I hadn't seen Nelson in maybe twelve years. We were never buddies, but we used to see each other around and were friendly. I always liked Danny, had a lot of respect for his brains and energy. I was glad to see him. First of all, I hadn't seen him for a long time, and secondly, his action now would help determine what I would do with Gloria Kirby.

Understand this: Danny Nelson didn't just walk into my office. With him it was a production. His entrance was preceded by two thugs, big boys and rough-looking. Then came Danny, dapper and smiling. Bringing up the rear was another guy, even bigger than the first two. The company formed a backward triangle with Danny in the middle.

Manny Green was impressed by the performance, and a little awed. He sat there with his mouth open and a card halfway between his hand and the pack.

Nelson was smiling at me. "Hello, Johnny. Long time no see."

"Yeah. Long time. You look good for yourself, Danny."

"Feel good," he said. He hit his stomach with his fist. "Hard as a rock. I keep in shape."

"I'm forgetting my manners," I said. "Danny, meet Manny. Mr. Green, Mr. Nelson." Manny closed his mouth and started to get up. One of Nelson's thugs pushed him back into the chair.

"I'm sorry to bust in this way, Johnny. I had a little business proposition I wanted your advice on. I think we'd better talk about it alone."

Manny said, "I'd be glad to get out of here. Only this guy won't let me stand up."

"Let him go, boys," Danny said.

"I'll keep the score, Manny. We'll settle up later." Manny didn't answer. He got out of there.

"Sorry I had to chase your friend out, Johnny, but I'm in kind of a hurry."

"What's on your mind?"

Nelson cased the room quickly and nodded toward the couch, and for a minute my heart was in my mouth. But it was only a signal to his boys. The three of them walked over and sat down on seventy thousand and fifty-three bucks, the fifty-three bucks being what the couch cost me secondhand. Danny sat in the chair near my desk.

"Johnny, I'm not standing on any ceremony with you. We understand each other, I think. We're the same kind of guys, you and me. I like you, Johnny. I always liked you even when you were a kid. I always wanted you to be part of the gang. You could have come a long way if you had stuck with the gang, but you wanted something different." He looked around the room, at the diploma hung on the wall. "You wanted this, and I got respect for you because you got it. Maybe it was as tough for you to get where you are as it was for me to get where I am. I don't know, Johnny. Either way it isn't easy, coming from where we did. There have been lots of times I thought of calling you in, Johnny, to help me out when I needed a guy with class and a good legal noodle. You know why I didn't?"

I didn't answer him. I just shook my head.

"Because I was scared. Imagine me scared! I was scared you'd turn me down, tell me you wouldn't want no part of a hoodlum. It would have made me feel bad, so I never did. You would have turned me down, wouldn't you, Johnny?"

"I think so, Danny. I made my decision a long time ago. I'm sticking with it."

"You can't turn me down now, Johnny. I didn't send for you, I'm coming to you. I'm asking you this as a pal. It's not nothing else."

"What do you want me to do?"

"Tell me where Gloria Kirby is."

I tried to look startled and then smiled. "Me tell *you?* I thought she was living with you."

"When is the last time you saw her?"

"It's a long time, Danny. We were shacked up together about ten years ago. I don't think I've seen her since. I've seen her picture plenty of times in the magazines and papers. You did a lot for her, Danny. She was a punk when I knew her. You made a glamour girl out of her."

"You wouldn't lie to me, Johnny?"

"What for? Why should I?"

"I don't know," he said. He shrugged his shoulders and looked around the room again. I hoped we had been careful in getting rid of evidence that Gloria had been there. I'd been a sap not to hide the dough more carefully. One false sit and a cushion might fall off the couch. "I don't know," Danny repeated, "I just got a feeling that she would have come to you." He looked up at me as though to explain. "We had kind of a fight this morning, me and Gloria. Just one of those things. So she packed up and left me. I've had time to think it over and I was wrong. I want her back. I was sitting around and thinking if I was Gloria Kirby where would I go under a similar circumstance. You know how you get to imagining things sometimes. Then I remembered that you and her used to live together in the old neighborhood. I remembered all the times she used to say to me, 'Johnny used to treat me good,' or 'Johnny never talked like that to me.' You know, Maguire, if I had a jealous streak I could have been plenty jealous of you the way Gloria kept throwing you up to me all the time. With me it was dough and excitement that kept her going. With you it was love."

"I never realized she felt that way. It wasn't like that when we lived together. We were just both sort of killing time, so we decided to do it together."

"You see how little a guy knows sometimes? You and her living together and you not even knowing how much she was in love with you." He shook his head slowly. "It's a funny world, Maguire, isn't it? Like when Gloria threatens to leave me. I don't think it'll ever happen. Then all of a sudden she does it and I feel bad. I really do, Johnny. I can get lots of dames. But Gloria is something special. You know that."

"Well, I haven't seen her, Danny. If she shows up I'll tell her to go back, that all is forgiven." I started to stand up to indicate that our business was over but Danny wasn't having any. He made himself more comfortable in the chair.

"Now, don't get mad at me, Johnny. This is nothing personal. But I got a feeling you're lying to me. I got a feeling that Gloria has been to see you today. She called you up, maybe, and told you to meet her somewhere. Maybe you ain't lying. Maybe you haven't seen her. Yet." He hit the word "yet" hard. "Maybe you've got a date to meet her later."

"You're wasting your time, Danny. I haven't seen her, I haven't heard from her, and I don't know where the hell she is."

"All right, Johnny, I told you not to get mad. I wasn't accusing you of nothing, I just said I got a feeling, that's all. I'm a guy who's got to go by what he feels. I never had no education or nothing like you did, I don't know how to figure things out according to the books. I got to go by what I feel, and I feel if I was Gloria Kirby I would have come to you if I was in trouble."

"You're wrong. This time your feelings have given you the wrong tip."

"You're a good-looking guy, Maguire. You got plenty of dames on the string, huh? Me, if I didn't have dough, there ain't a dame who would look at me twice. But you don't need dough. You got the face and the body. Do me a favor, pal. Don't let it get messed up."

"I take good care of myself."

"There was another guy—maybe you remember him. His name was Joey Nathan. Used to live in the old neighborhood, too. Did you know him?"

I shook my head.

"Good-looking guy. Had a nice wife and a family. But a smart guy, you know, a wise-guy type. Thought he could pull a fast one on me." Danny nodded toward the couch. "He didn't look so good when George over there got through with him. I went to the funeral and they didn't even have the coffin open."

"Which one," I asked, "is George?"

"The one at the end."

George was the biggest one, the rear guard. He was smiling at me. I definitely did not like the type. His teeth were tobacco-stained, his skin was yellowish and greasy, and his blond hair was plastered flat to his head. His eyes were big and baby blue, watery-looking and almost transparent. I smiled and waved to him. "Hello, George."

This time Danny cut in and his voice was no longer gentle and understanding. "I ain't got time for comedians, Maguire. Cut the funny stuff and tell me what you know."

This time I stood up and stayed up. "Look, Danny, I'll take so much from you for old times' sake. But this is enough. I told you I don't know where Gloria Kirby is. Now I've got work to do."

"You won't look so pretty all messed up, Johnny."

"And in case you haven't heard, I don't scare easy. Maybe I moved out of the old neighborhood, but I learned how to take care of myself there and I haven't forgotten it, any of it. Now, take the Andrews Sisters and get the hell out of here."

"Don't get mad, Johnny. You Irishers are all alike. You got tempers that go off so fast."

"Get out, Danny."

He stood up and the three thugs stood up with him. "Let me have the needle, Fred." One of the men handed him a needle, just like the one Gloria had. "You know what this is, Maguire?"

"Sure."

"Gloria needs this. She didn't have much with her. She can't live without it. You see, that's why I ain't too worried about her coming back to me." He handed it back to Fred. Smart boy, this Danny. He would never risk having the stuff found on him at any time. "Gloria is no good without dope any more. She's got to have it. The only place she can get it is from me, and sooner or later she'll come crawling back begging for a shot of it. You know what I'm going to do?"

"What are you going to do?"

"I'm going to hold it about this far from her arm, and before I give it to her I'm going to ask her a lot of questions. Questions like where she went and what she did and who she saw. Who she saw, Johnny. I'm going to make her tell me everybody she saw, everybody who she came to for help."

"So what?"

"She's going to be squirming, Johnny. Did you ever see a dope fiend squirm for the stuff? Terrible sight. I'd seen it maybe a thousand times, and every time I get a creepy feeling all over. They ain't got no self-will, they let everything come out. They can't hold back nothing they promised not to say. So Gloria is going to tell me everything. She won't want to, maybe, but she won't be able to help herself. You know what, Maguire?"

I was being a straight man but I didn't care. "What, Danny?"

"I hope she don't mention your name. I really do. I'd hate to think that an old buddy would lie to me."

"Don't make yourself sick worrying about it. She won't mention my name."

"If she does, Johnny, I'm warning you now, sentiment ain't a part of my make-up. You'll get yours and it won't be quick and it won't be pretty. You understand?" He waited for an answer. "You sure, now, you haven't seen Gloria Kirby today? You sure you ain't got something to tell me?"

"I've got nothing to say to you, Danny. Nothing."

"Once I walk out that door, it's too late. You know that."

"Walk out," I said. "I've got nothing to be afraid of."

The two advance guards walked into the hall. Nelson hesitated at the door. "Funny thing," he said. "I had a hunch about you. A feeling that Gloria would get in touch with you. I'm never wrong. Am I, George?" George smiled with his yellow teeth and shook his head. "There's always a first time, eh, Johnny?"

"Yeah, Danny," I said. "Always a first time."

Danny Nelson exited smiling. I waited until I heard the elevator door open and close then I made a beeline for the whisky bottle and had myself a long, long swig.

CHAPTER FOUR

Okay, I was scared. Nelson played for keeps. He was a man of his word; good or bad, he stuck to a promise. And he had promised to kill me. He was right about Gloria's needing the dope. I should have realized that, I shouldn't have paid any attention to what she said about tapering off and getting along without it. My damn heart keeps getting in the way of my thinking and it winds me up behind the eight ball.

The dough was there, still under the couch. I figured I'd better find a good place to hide it. Gloria Kirby had her confession, spilling the beans about the rackets, to protect her life. I had two things to protect mine. Nelson wouldn't touch me until Gloria Kirby showed up, and even if she showed up he wouldn't kill me until he found out where the money was. He wouldn't kill me, but his boy George would mess me up plenty. Of that I was positive.

The seats of the couch were still warm from where the three thugs had parked their behinds. I scooped up the dough and rammed it in my brief case and went down to Tina's office. It was just about quitting time. The girl who worked for her had her hat on and said hello and good-by in one sentence.

Tina was banging away like crazy on the typewriter. "Of all days," she said, "to be stuck with this and I absolutely have to get it out. You'll have to put up with rough elbows tonight, Johnny. I simply won't have time to polish them like it says in all the glamour magazines. Will you love me less because my elbows are rough?"

"Baby, one part of you that interests me not at all are your elbows."

"You'll have to give me a lift, darling. I left my car home. Sit down and amuse yourself while I finish this up."

There was a newspaper on Phyllis' desk. I sat down, lighted a cigarette, and began reading the paper. It was there, the whole story about the seventy thousand dollars. It didn't make sense. The story blamed the robbery on a young bank teller from Ohio, Sanford Wharton III. A very fancy name for a bank teller. There was a picture of him splashed across the front page and the kid was behind bars. The paper said they believed the money to be hidden in the teller's apartment. That Nelson boy was quite an engineer to arrange this one.

"Tina, when did you get this newspaper?"

"What newspaper?"

I shoved it in front of her face. "This one!"

She knocked it out of the way and went on with her typing. "Phyllis must have got it when she went out for coffee. It was about four o'clock."

"Can you close your ears for about five minutes?"

"I don't even have time to listen."

"Promise you won't ask any questions about anything you hear?"

"Of course I promise. Damn it, Johnny, you made me make a mistake." She riffled through the carbons and began making erasures.

I sat down at Phyllis' desk and dialed the number of the local FBI. Luckily my friend Wally Forrester hadn't left yet. Wally and I had been through law school together. We were alike in many ways, both unattached and on the prowl. When I get fed up with dames and married people depress me, I call up Wally Forrester and we weep into a little beer together.

"Glad to hear from you, Maguire. Just happen to have a free evening. It's a perfect night to be hoisting a few."

"Wally, I never ask you favors, do I?"

"You need dough?"

"No, I don't need dough. I need information."

"About what?"

"About a robbery. The City Federal Bank. Seventy grand. They've got a kid locked up. Confessed the whole thing. But I got a hunch there's going to be something missing when they put the whole thing together. You got enough influence to find out the details of the confession? I'd like to know why he stole the dough, if he's involved anyone else, and what he did with it."

"Seems to me the federal government insures banks against something or other. I ought to be able to bluff my way into the police department on that."

"I'd appreciate it. And keep me out of it. You don't know me and you never heard of me."

"This doesn't sound like my drinking partner. What's it all about, or isn't it any of my business?"

"It's got something to do with a client of mine. Just keep it under your hat."

"O.K., Johnny, my boy. How do I get in touch with you?"

"I'll wait here for your call." I gave him Tina's office number. "If I don't answer the phone myself, hang up and I'll get in touch with you later."

After I hung up I realized that it had been awfully quiet in the room. Tina had stopped typing and was watching me. "Johnny," she began.

"You said you weren't going to ask any questions."

"I know, but—"

"But nothing, baby. No questions."

"I can't finish this damn thing. I'll have to get down early in the morning and finish it before nine. Wait here. I'm going down the hall and powder my nose."

Tina's office was as good a hiding place as any. There was a closet full of stationery supplies. I picked out an envelope box, half filled. I put the money in there and put the box under a lot of other boxes. It was kind of a dirty trick to play on Tina, hiding the money within her reach, but I didn't think it was safe to carry it out of the building. Ten to one Nelson would have a tail on me, following me around everywhere.

During the time that it took Tina to powder her nose, I made some fast decisions. I was going to take Tina to the dance. Being sure that Nelson was going to know every movement of mine, I thought it would be best to go ahead and do what I was going to do anyway. I'd go to the dance and then take Tina home, go upstairs with her, and to all appearances spend the night. At least, I was going to walk out of the building with her the next morning as though I had spent the night.

It was important to get Gloria Kirby out of town before anything happened. I was going to have to figure out a way to get some dope to shoot into her. I knew I would be taking a hell of a chance riding out of town with her, but the odds were better than leaving her alone in the hotel room and giving her a chance to get desperate enough to go crawling back to Nelson.

Tina came back and began getting ready to go home. The telephone rang and I jumped at it.

"I got what I could on the kid, Johnny. It's not much. He's not the talkative kind. His name is Sanford Wharton III. Comes from Ohio. Good family. Lots of dough. Took a job at the bank to learn the banking business. Says he stole the dough because he needed it." Wally laughed. "He needs it. We could use it, too."

"I wouldn't know what to do with it," I said. "What else?"

"No trace of the dough. The guy says he got scared and burned it. Don't make sense, does it?"

"It sure doesn't. Does he say he was in this with anyone?"

"No. Says he did it all alone. They've checked his friends, tried to find out who he buddies around with. Seems they've run into the best people in town. Very posh crowd. He must be an awful jerk, this kid. He couldn't possibly get away with it. As soon as they found it missing they went right to him. Handling that dough was in his department. Such a jerk I don't understand."

"Anything else?"

"Nothing else," he said. "Not a thing. From the way they're talking down at the Police Department, this is already yesterday's news. If the kid had murdered somebody, at least he might have kept hitting the front pages for a couple of days. Maybe he's off his nut or something. I don't know."

"Thanks a million. If there's ever anything I can do to repay you, Wally, you know that all you got to do is whistle."

He whistled.

"O.K., shoot. What do you want?"

s

"O.K. I'll drop you and go on to my place, get dressed, and come back for you. This is formal, isn't it?"

"You have to wear your pretty white coat, darling. Is it clean?"

"Jesus, I don't know. I don't even know where it is."

"You need a wife, Counselor, to remember all these little things for you."

"I got a better idea. I should never go formal. That would solve everything."

"Your memory is very short, Johnny. Do you remember last summer, the same dance?"

I shook my head. I didn't remember anything. I had been going to these dances for five years and they were all alike, all filled with over-plump housewives and overready stenographers.

"Last year you got stinking drunk. A friend of yours brought a bottle of Irish whisky."

"Oh, now I remember."

"You don't remember passing out, do you? Or getting sick? Do you remember whose cool hand held your furrowed forehead?"

"O.K., so I got drunk. What's that got to do with my suit?"

"You suit has been cleaned and is hanging in my closet. Your shirt has been washed and starched and lies in the bottom drawer among my bras."

"Is there room?"

"Don't be vulgar. Your size thirteen patent leathers are right beside my size sixes. In other words, Counselor, you don't have to go home. You can get dressed at my place."

"I've got a razor there, haven't I?"

"My apartment is full of all sort of debris of yours, so come along, Counselor. I'm not taking any chances of letting you out of my sight. And while I'm luxuriating in my bath, you can fix my toaster. It's on the blink again."

I walked up to her. "I'll fix your toaster, all right."

She saw what I was up to. "Johnny, don't you dare! Johnny, stop it! Johnny, your hands are cold. Stop it! Johnny!"

I withdrew smiling. "You asked me to fix your—"

"Never mind my toaster," she said. "I'll take it to a repair shop."

CHAPTER FIVE

At first, I thought it was imagination. There were two hundred and fifty other guys in and around the ballroom. Why me? Then I saw her staring at me again as she danced by with some character old enough to be her father. Our eyes caught but she looked quickly away.

This was not an ordinary girl. She didn't belong at a ward heeler's clambake. This was daisy-chain stuff. She was about five-three in her shoes. The dress she was wearing must have cost plenty. It was pale green lace, a lot of green lace, except at the top, where there wasn't anything much, only a thin filmy scarf of the same pale green. How she ever got a dress the same color as her eyes I'll never know, but there it was, and it was topped off with a mass of the most beautiful red hair I ever hoped to run my fingers through. She wasn't like a lot of redheads. Her hair was soft and finely textured.

I lost sight of her again as she danced toward the center of the floor. I wasn't worried. By then I was convinced she had something on her mind, something to do with me, and would be back. It was possible that she was giving me the eye for the same reason I was giving the eye back to her, because this was something special to go home with. But I rejected that idea almost right away. A girl like that doesn't have to prowl for men. Then I thought she might have something to do with Vic. Vic was the guy I had called from Tina's apartment to see if he could get hold of some dope to feed to Gloria.

As much as you can trust a dope peddler, I trusted Vic. He owed me a couple of favors and I knew that in a pinch he could keep his mouth shut. That was the important thing. I told him what I wanted and told him not to ask any questions and if anybody asked him any questions he didn't know a thing; mainly, he didn't know me.

The plan was this: He was going to show up at the dance and somehow pass me a vial of the stuff. If anything looked dangerous to him, if one of Danny's boys were around or anything like that, he was going to put a flower in his buttonhole and I would stay away and we would make other arrangements later.

The dance had been going on for a couple of hours and I hadn't seen any sign of him yet. As a matter of fact, I had seen very little of Tina since we got there. We had danced the first dance together and then someone cut in and she had been dancing ever since with a stream of men from fifteen to seventy-five. Once in a while she'd waltz by the table and wave to me or wrinkle up her nose. I was planning on giving her a bad time when we got home. She put up a hullabaloo about my almost not taking her to the dance and then, when we finally got there, she didn't pay any attention to me.

I was thinking that this redheaded girl had something to do with Vic, that he had sent her instead of coming himself. It was farfetched to think of this girl and Vic in the same breath, but you can never tell. Dope brings many kinds of people incongruously together.

Also it went through my head that this girl might have something to do with Danny Nelson. Nelson was smart. He wasn't through with me yet, not by a long shot. Maybe he was baiting the hook with redheaded bait. That was a very real possibility. If she was bait, I might nibble around a little, but I sure as hell wasn't going to bite.

Or maybe she was nothing. Maybe it was my imagination and she was just a girl at a dance and I'd never see her again.

Whatever it was, I knew that I couldn't do anything about it. I had to sit it out and see if anything happened, to see if Vic showed and if this girl really was going to make a try for me.

Tina came over after a while, perspiring a little and looking slightly disheveled. "Johnny, I've been so worried you're not having a good time."

"Me? I'm having a swell time. Real peachy."

"Darling, I'm sorry, but I've been getting such a rush, and when a girl's past twenty-one she has to take advantage of every opportunity."

"Past what?"

"I didn't say how far past, did I? Besides, I promised myself I wasn't going to start worrying until I was thirty." She brushed some hair in place. "You see, I don't really have too much time, so I'm having fun while I can."

"If I wasn't around, you wouldn't have any worries at all, would you?"

"Darling, I love to worry about you."

"I don't mean that. You'd be married long ago if I wasn't around. I always get in the way."

She leaned over and kissed me full on the mouth, hard and with heft behind it. "I like you in the way," she said. "Now I've got to powder my nose."

Almost as soon as she was gone, the red-haired girl in the green dress came near the table. She looked for a minute as though she were going to walk right up to me, then she changed her direction and walked away. She let go of the scarf that had covered her shoulders. It floated to the floor and fell near me. I picked it up fast and took off after her, knowing all the time that she might be a trap, a deliberately set Danny Nelson trap. I didn't care. I followed her anyway.

The girl moved swiftly through the fringe of people along the edge of the dance floor. I lost sight of her as she weaved in and out of the dancing couples, but then I caught a flash of that red hair disappearing behind the bandstand and I half ran to catch up with her. There was a doorway behind the orchestra leading out to the terrace. She was there waiting for me, her back to me, her hands clutching the iron railing and her head raised toward the black, starless night.

I stood behind her without moving. I was aware of the scarf in my hand, the soft texture of it and the fragrance of it, the same fragrance her shoulders had as I put the flimsy wisp of fabric around her. "You smell just like a girl I used to know," I said.

She knew I was standing there. Neither my movement nor the sound of my voice had startled her. She pulled the scarf around her tightly. There was a beginning coolness blowing in through the warmth of the night. The filmy scarf was little protection against it. Her shoulders hunched together and there was a shiver rippling through the muscles of her naked back. I took off my white coat and put it over her shoulders. I lighted a cigarette and put it in her mouth. Then I lighted one for myself.

When I spoke my voice came out in a heavy whisper. It was the way the night was, meant to be whispered into, not meant to carry the hard, clear sounds of the day. "You're supposed to say thank you to the man. Turn around and say thank you."

"Thank you," she said softly. She didn't turn around.

I was thinking what a perfect setup this was. This was the way to end the loneliness and the emptiness. This was the night to meet a girl, this kind of girl. This girl. It was a perfect setup. For one minute I closed my eyes against the night, and without touching her, just knowing she was there, I was feeling something pretty close to wonderful. It was as close as I had been in a long, long time.

Then I opened my eyes and it was over, the feeling was gone. It was *too* perfect. This girl didn't want me. She wanted something else, something I had or something I knew. It wasn't because I did to her what she did to me. I snapped out of it and remembered I was a big boy now, and I was supposed to be a tough one.

"O.K., Red," I said. "This is real cozy, very romantic. The night is young, you're beautiful, and I'm a sucker. So tell me what the pitch is."

"Go away. Please go away and leave me alone." Her voice was right for the night. Low and husky, sounding the way the wind does coming through thickness of leaves or sweeping low through tall grass. I had to hold tight again and keep remembering that this was a setup, too perfect to be happening without a hitch.

"What kind of game are you playing, Red? First you want me and then you don't. You didn't go to all the trouble of luring me out here just to send me away again, did you? Or maybe that's all you were supposed to do, get me out here. Is Danny Nelson hiding behind one of those potted palms waiting to put a bullet through my head?"

I saw her flinch when I said Nelson's name. But her voice was calm and soft-sounding. "Please go away."

I took her by the shoulder and turned her roughly around so that she was facing me. There were those eyes, those wonderful cat-green eyes, looking up at me. I was mixed up. Maybe I had figured her wrong. She was frightened, really frightened. Her eyes were alive and afire with fear. And there was a quivering in her lower lip. So easy to stop. My mouth against her mouth and the quivering would stop and there would be the taste of her lips and the wetness of her mouth. I started to lean forward to touch her lips.

But this was business. I had to keep telling myself that. This was business and maybe it was going to mean lives. I caught myself halfway to her mouth. "Nice try, Red. I almost fell. Mighty tempting. You've got to be a man of iron. Tell Danny Nelson you did your best but I didn't fall. Tell him almost, but not quite."

"You're hurting me." I guess I was holding her pretty hard. I eased up a little. "I don't know Danny Nelson," she said. "I don't know what you're talking about. Please, please go away."

"You got me out here for a reason. I'm not going away until I find out what that reason is."

"I didn't. I swear I didn't. I didn't even realize I had dropped my stole until you brought it to me. There isn't any more to it than that. I don't know what all these things are about, the things you're saying to me. Really I don't. Now, please go away."

"You deny that you've been giving me the once-over all evening?"

She lowered her head. "I did look at you," she said. "I thought you were someone else at first." She looked up at me and quickened the tempo of her speaking. "I thought you were someone I used to know."

I shook my head. "Old line, Red. Out of date. Not convincing. Try something else."

This time she tried to break my hold on her and getaway. I held fast. "What's the matter? Didn't Nelson dope you up enough to give you guts to go all the way through with this?"

"Through with what? What are you talking about? I don't know anybody named Danny Nelson. Now, let me go."

I wouldn't let her go. I held her chin up so that her eyes had to look at me, look into my eyes. She stared at me, bewildered and frightened. Suddenly her eyes closed and her head fell back. "All right," she whispered. "I give up." My arms went around her to steady her. "I did want you out here. But it's not what you think. I swear it isn't. Danny Nelson didn't make me do this. I hate Danny Nelson. I hate him. I wanted you out here because—I thought that maybe you could—" She was having a hell of a time saying what she was trying to say. Or she was a good actress. I couldn't lose sight of that possibility. All of this might have been part of the trap.

I whispered down into that wonderful, soft red hair. "What did you think I could do? Huh?"

"Oh, what's the use? It won't do any good to tell you. You can't help me. No one can help me. I'll have to do it alone."

"Tell me, Red,"

"No, no, please. Let me go."

"You're going to tell me. I'm not budging and neither are you until you tell me why you got me out here."

This time is was her turn to look me in the eye. "Nothing will do any good unless you believe that Danny Nelson has nothing to do with this. I don't deny I know him. I do know him and I hate him. I hate what he's done. You've got to believe that he doesn't even know that I'm here. Believe that. Please. You've got to."

I couldn't believe it. I couldn't afford to believe it. This wasn't a game you could play for worn-out Dewey buttons. Seventy grant and people's lives were involved. My life, too. I couldn't afford to believe her. I never under-estimated Nelson. He was clever enough to put this girl up to what she was doing, outlining every action in advance for her, even to the look in her eyes, honest and pleading and hard to reject.

"Supposing I did believe you, Red. What then? What would happen after that?"

"But you don't believe me. I can see that. It's not use supposing. You've got to really believe me. You've just got to."

I shook my head.

"I knew it was no use," she said. "I knew it the minute you came out here. That's why I wanted you to go away. I knew you wouldn't help. I knew you couldn't." Then it started, a dribble of tears she tried bravely to hold back. To some men tears mean nothing. So she's crying, they think. I'm built different. When a dame cries, something inside me goes to pieces. I can't help it.

"Easy, Red. Take it easy. Jesus, there's only so much a man can take without melting. Don't cry. For God's sake, don't cry. If you're like this, I'll have to be Sir Galahad. And you know what that will make me? Dead, baby. A big, dead Irishman."

She started to say something but her words were cut off by the sound of a gunshot. One single shot had been fired into the night and it had come from close by. In one quick move I picked up the redhead and bolted over the iron railing and landed on the soft ground in the middle of a lot of landscaping. There was a sound of running on the terrace. One man. When he was almost directly in line in front of us, there were two more shots. The man spun around, straightened up for a minute, and then fell to the hard, stone terrace floor. He lay there, motionless.

Through the bushes I could see enough to recognize the man. It was Vic, the dope peddler. And there was a red carnation in his buttonhole.

Danger!

From what? From the girl huddled beside me? Or from the hand holding the gun? I didn't know. The only thing I knew was that I didn't want to be found anywhere near Vic. I didn't want anyone to know Vic was there to meet me.

A crowd gathered quickly. As soon as the confusion was great enough and the noise loud enough, I led the girl out of the bushes and we ran out on the golf course and took refuge in a deep sand trap. "You all right, baby?"

"I think so. I guess I tore my dress."

"Lucky that's all."

"It was horrible to see that. I've—I've never seen a man killed before."

"It was like I was saying, in whatever you're mixed up in, there's lots of killing. Maybe you'd better forget the whole thing."

"I can't. I wish I could. I wish none of this had ever happened."

"Come on, Red, you might as well tell me."

"Look at your coat. It's full of mud."

"Don't worry about the coat. Tell me what you're mixed up in."

She said it straight out. "I have to find Gloria Kirby."

It was as if someone had handed a good one right on my jaw. After what had happened, I was ready to believe this girl, believe that she wasn't a front for Danny Nelson. I thought to myself, What a sap you are, Maguire.

"O.K., Red. Beat it. And tell Danny that not even you—and you're pretty terrific—can make me tell something I don't know. Tell Danny I don't know where Gloria Kirby is. Tell him he put the best convincer on the case I ever saw. If I had anything to say, Red, there's no one I'd rather say it to. But I don't know anything. You understand that?"

Slowly she stood up and took off my coat. She straightened out her dress and smoothed back her hair. "If you don't know where Gloria Kirby is, then it doesn't matter what you think. It doesn't matter if you think I'm working for Danny Nelson or not."

"Tell me something. Why do you want Gloria Kirby?"

"Never mind," she said. Her voice had a beaten sound to it. "It doesn't matter. I'll find her. Somehow. I have to."

"What made you think I would know where she is?"

"Danny Nelson thinks you know. So I thought I'd try."

"You know, for someone who says she isn't palsy with Mr. Nelson, you seem to know a hell of a lot about his private thinking."

"I'm sorry I put you to all this trouble." She started to leave.

"Look, you can't just run away. I don't even know your name."

"My name doesn't matter. You'll probably never see me again."

"But I want to see you again."

This time, with no warning, she climbed out of the sand trap and began running toward the clubhouse. I went after her. She ran pretty good for a girl. I caught her and held her still so that I could look into those wonderful green eyes. "Listen, Red, maybe I'm wrong about you and maybe I'm not. I'm not as much of a heel as you think I am. I'd help you if I could. You've got to believe that."

She looked up at me. She was a picture of wide-eyed innocence. I was thinking maybe I was being an awful hardhearted jerk. "I do believe you," she said. "Now, let me go, please."

"Maybe when this is over, Red—maybe when you've found what you're looking for or have done what you're trying to do—maybe then we can try again. I mean, maybe we can get together and pretend like tonight didn't happen." I let go of her shoulders.

"Maybe," she said, and then she didn't say any more. I didn't chase her this time. I let her go. I was content to watch her as she walked away from me, all those yards of green lace billowing in the wind, that flaming hair, and all that wonderful girl.

Vic was dead and it was my fault and there would be no dope to shoot into Gloria Kirby's arm. I had to get her far away and quickly before she broke down, before she did anything foolish. Like telling Danny Nelson that I was being the All-American Boy, sticking my damn Mick neck out a mile to help a derelict woman.

CHAPTER SIX

I made a mental note to tell Nelson he ought to hire a guy who really knows how to tail a man without telegraphing it. I picked up the headlights of a car as we were pulling out of the driveway of the country club and the car was sticking like glue behind me.

"Every year," Tina was saying, "it's something else. Last year you got sick all over it and this year you decide to roll all over the golf course in it. It's nice to know you're so rich you can afford to throw a white coat away every time you wear it."

"When you have to foot the bills, you can squawk. Until then, shut up!"

"Besides that, who were you rolling around in a sand trap with?" She brushed some sand off the coat. "I can't take my eyes off you for two minutes but you're off somewhere with some—"

"What are you talking about? You didn't give me a tumble from the time we got there. You were carrying on with every two-bit political bum in town."

"Dancing, darling. I was dancing. That's quite different from what you were doing. You could write a book, Johnny. 'Fun in a Sand Trap,' or 'I Must Have Forgotten My Niblick.' You'd have an instant best-seller."

"This was business. I told you before. Business."

Tina laughed. "You were so busy with your business you missed a first-class murder."

"Who?"

"I don't know. It was very exciting. Some man. Nobody seemed to know who he was or who shot him." Her brow furrowed. "Heavens, Johnny, you didn't shoot him, did you?"

"Hell, no."

"You get mixed up in so many things, I'm never quite sure. You didn't have anything to do with it at all?"

I didn't answer her so she let it pass and lighted a cigarette, and the rest of the ride back to Tina's apartment was made in a cold silence.

The headlights that had followed us all the way stopped a half block behind Tina's apartment building. When Tina saw I was getting out with her, she said, "You don't have to get out, Johnny. Go ahead. I'll get in all right."

"I'm coming up."

"You are?"

"Yeah."

"That's nice." But she didn't move.

I gave her a light whack on the fanny. "Come on, move it."

"I don't want to be difficult, darling, but I'm not in the mood." She smiled. "You know what I mean, not in the mood?" Then she laughed, not very pleasantly. "But then, how could you? You're always in the mood. You never care who it is or where it is or what it is. You're always in the mood."

"Yak, yak, yak."

"I can overlook when you've been with someone the night before. It's hard, but I do manage to be overcome enough with your charm to overlook it. But when I have been preceded by someone just an hour before, I get out of the mood. I draw the line."

"Look, Tina, nothing happened on the golf course.And I got something else to tell you. Nothing is going to happen upstairs. We're being tailed. We're going upstairs looking just like we're headed for the sack. You can go to bed. I'm going to change clothes, get out the back way, get into your car, and drive away."

"To that erstwhile blonde?"

"Yeah. I'm going to get her out of town before she decides to tell all her troubles to a certain character."

This time she was serious. Worried and serious. "Johnny, why can't you stay out of trouble? I'm going to be an old woman worrying about you."

"You'd be bored stiff if I was the steady type. Now, come on. I've got to move fast."

In the elevator she said, "What if they see you coming out of the building? What if they follow you?"

"They won't. And they won't see me coming back."

"You're coming back? What time?"

I shook my head. "It'll be too late. You'll be fast asleep."

"Wake me up."

"Now look who's in the mood." She gave me a kick in the shins. But not very hard.

It wasn't hard getting out of there. I figured a tail dumb enough to give himself away wouldn't be smart enough to watch any car but mine. I drove downtown in Tina's car in a very roundabout way, just in case my shadow wasn't as dumb as I thought. But there was no sign of anyone. It looked clean as a whistle behind me.

Even late at night, the hotel lobby was crowded and noisy. I was just another guy going up to his room. The hall on the seventeenth floor was empty. I went right to Gloria's room as if I belonged there. A "Do Not Disturb" sign had been hung on the door. I left it there, opened the door, and went inside quickly.

I knew it instantly. I knew it without having to turn on the lights. The blackness and the quiet of the room were the blackness and the quiet of death. My heart had sunk before I touched the light switch; my eyes closed automatically at the click of the switch. It was a couple of seconds before I opened them to the brightness and the death of the room.

She lay on the threshold between the bathroom and bedroom. She had fallen with her arms outstretched and there was a circle of blood around each hand. I stood without moving, stunned by what I saw and shocked by it nonetheless for knowing how it would be.

I saw the note on the bed. I didn't want to read it. I didn't want to know what her last words were. My insides were wrung out, exhausted. They couldn't take much more. They couldn't take whatever she had said in that note on the bed.

There was nothing to do and there was a lot to do. When the police found her, they couldn't find Gloria Kirby. They would have to find Marion Talbot of New York City. I took my time, tried to be calm, tried to think of everything. I removed every label from her few clothes, so that there would be no chance of tracing her. I watched where my hands touched and wiped off any prints my fingers left.

All the time I worked around the bedroom, I didn't look at the note on the bed. I'm glad I was alone in there. I was behaving like a big, goddamn sissy. I closed my eyes as I stepped over her and went into the bathroom. The things Tina had bought for her were spilled out of the little bag. It was going to look funny when the police saw them; everything was new and unused. There were no drugstore stickers on any of the items, so it would be hard to find out where they had been purchased.

On the sink was the opened package of razor blades. It was a damn peculiar thing for Tina to have bought. Then I spotted the razor and shaving cream, my brand of shaving cream. The same kind of razor and the same kind of shaving cream were in Tina's medicine chest.

I had used them earlier that evening. This was Tina's sense of humor. She had put them in with Gloria's things as a joke for me. Some joke: But I realized that if the razor blades hadn't been there, Gloria would have found another way. With people who want to die there's always another way.

When there was nothing left to do but read the note,I walked over to the window and looked out. The lights of the cars made a snaky pattern along the broad drive fringing the lake. The lake itself was dark and calm.

I was wondering how long it would take before Danny Nelson found out that Gloria Kirby was dead. That he would find it out I was certain. Yet as far as I knew there could be no tracing the girl who lay dead on the floor. Maybe Nelson would never know that someone namedMarion Talbot had committed suicide in the Stevens Hotel. To all appearances, it was just another suicide worth a couple of lines in the newspapers. It was bad publicity for the hotel and maybe they would have enough pull to keep it out of the papers altogether so Danny would never know and Gloria Kirby would be buried in the city yard, unmarked and unclaimed. The fabulous Gloria Kirby, who had everything in the world. And who had nothing.

I thought of the possibility that Nelson would have the city morgue cased. But it would be one of his stooges on the job, and it wasn't likely he would recognize Gloria with her hair dyed black, the glamour washed off, and the pallor and agony of death distorting her face.

How long would it be before Danny found out that Gloria was dead? I wasn't sure if it would be that night or maybe not for six months. Meanwhile, I had a boxful of dough and Nelson wanted it and I had to decide how to get rid of it so that Danny would never, never know I had had it.

Without looking at it, I picked up the note and crushed it into my pocket. I checked the room again to see if I had left anything undone, I took the key out of my pocket, wiped the prints off it, and threw it on the floor. With my handkerchief over my hand, I flicked off the lights, opened and closed the door, walked to the elevator, got out of the hotel, and drove Tina's car back to her place.

I parked on a side street and jimmied a window to get in the back way. Not taking a chance of anyone's watching the front elevator, I climbed up the seven flights to Tina's apartment. She was fast asleep and didn't awaken when I walked in. I smiled to myself when I saw she was wearing the black lace nightgown I had bought her for Mother's Day.

In the bathroom I stripped off my clothes and stood under a hot shower for a long time, not thinking about anything, not remembering anything, not planning anything. I was aware only of the hotness of the shower and the depth of the steam and the way it felt against my body.

The mirror had become clouded. I opened the bathroom door a crack to let some of the steam out. The cool air from the bedroom chilled me and I grabbed a towel and rubbed myself dry. I took my time about folding the towel and putting it carefully back in place. My clothes, too, I arranged carefully on the hook on the back of the door. Then, when it was all done, I took the note Gloria had written, sat down on the edge of the tub and read it.

Johnny—

Don't be sorry for me. I had everything and I lost it and I got it back again. That doesn't happen very often. I'm lucky. I had you twice.

Don't be sorry for anything. I'm no good, no good for anyone or for myself. Except for that quick hour when we loved each other again. I was good then. I hope Danny rots. I hope you find everything you want. Love a girl who's clean and good and worthy of your love. In a little while, I'll be like that. I'll stop being a tramp. The house in the country would never have worked. Danny would have got me. He can't get me now.

There was no signature, just those words. I found a match, lighted it, and touched it to the paper. When the flame burned near my fingers, I let the paper drop into the washbowl and burn out. I turned on the faucets and let the swirl of water wash the ashes down the drain.

Perspiration had burst out all over my body. I took the towel and wiped myself dry again. Then I went into the bedroom. As I stood near the bed watching Tina sleep, my bare feet touched something soft on the floor. I leaned over and picked up the black lace nightgown and ran the softness of it through my hands as though it were sand. The green lace dress had felt like this, too. And her wonderful red hair as it brushed against my face had been silky and fleetingly soft like this.

But this was black lace, still warm from body heat. And the hair on the pillow was dark. The closed eyes were feigning sleep.

Love, I was thinking, is many things. It was the frantic, hungry, uncontrolled passion on the floor of a hotel room. That, in a way, was love. And love was meeting a girl in the night, making you want to whisper soft words. That love made your body come alive with a softness and deliciousness of taste and touch. It wasn't only the vital part of you that was alive with this love; every part of you was knowing love and wanting love. That kind of love.

Love, I was thinking, is many things. Then I lifted the thin cover and got into bed beside Tina.

CHAPTER SEVEN

The next morning, I fixed Tina's toaster. We took our time over breakfast until Tina remembered the work she had left unfinished the day before; then we hurried. Nelson's tail man was still on the job when we came out of the building. He followed us all the way to the parking lot next to the office. I told Tina I would call her later and she went to her office and I went up to mine.

My office had been given the business. Everything was torn apart, strewn around the room. I wasn't surprised. Nelson had a hunch about me and he was trying to prove his hunch. He would know by now that Tina and I were involved together. I dialed her office immediately to make sure that they hadn't torn her place up. It was O.K. Nothing had happened, but I figured I'd move the money to a new hiding place later just in case they decided to pay a return visit.

I sent the elevator man down for the newspapers to see if they were carrying the story of Gloria's suicide yet. There was nothing in that edition. Almost the whole front page was devoted to the shooting of Vic Domotti at the country club. There were plenty of pictures. It was good copy. They had found a vial of dope in Vic's pocket. One of the papers dragged up a lot of old material on dope peddling in the city and all the evils of it. Their theory was that it was a gangland killing, one dope mob getting even with another.

On an inside page both papers carried a follow-up story on the bank robbery and the young man who had stolen seventy thousand dollars. Wally Forrester was wrong about its being only one day's news. It seems the police were not convinced that he had burned the dough. The Chief of Police had a theory that he was mixed up with a woman and had passed the money on to her. I knew how the Chief carried on when he got a theory. He'd have the boys working day and night, right around the clock.

It was a new wrinkle. Maybe Gloria had been feeding me a line about the house in the country. Maybe Danny was smelling the right rat. Maybe there was a guy she was doing this for, only it wasn't like she told me. This kid in the bank steals the dough according to Nelson's plan. He doesn't turn the dough over to Nelson. He gives it to Gloria instead. Both of them pulled the double cross on Danny.

Maybe. There were a hell of a lot of maybes involved, and in the meantime I was sitting with the dough and I was looking like the guy Gloria most wanted to run away with.

I figured that the most expedient thing for me to do was have a talk with the bank teller who was sitting in jail. There were little confidences that had to be exchanged between him and me. If I knew the whole story, the real story, it might help me. I thought I might even be able to involve Nelson directly. A lot of people would be happy about that. The trick was going to be to get in to see him so that no one knew it was I. I couldn't let Nelson know I was wise to his connection with the missing money.

I phoned Wally Forrester again at the FBI. He didn't sound so good when he answered the phone. "What's the matter, Wally, did you break your back?"

"Maguire, I would rather not talk to you after what happened."

"What happened?"

"What happened, you ask? That girl. Damn it, I think she is your aunt."

"Tell me. What happened?"

"Everything. Everything happened. Except…"

"Except what?"

"You guessed it, Maguire. Everything happened but what I wanted to happen."

I started to laugh.

"Sure, go ahead and laugh. It didn't cost you sixty bucks. First she's hungry. All right, so she's hungry. But not just hungry, this girl. Like she hasn't eaten for two weeks she eats. Do I care? No. I figure this is something very terrific. I figure Maguire has been here, and where Maguire is, there is something terrific. So she eats until there isn't any more room to put anything else. Then you know what she wants to do? She wants to dance. All right, so we go dancing. After an hour it's enough already. But you think that she wants to—"

I broke in. "You mean you didn't get it?"

"Indigestion I got. Sore feet I got. A hangover I got something terrible. Everything I got but what I was after."

"Tough luck, Wally. Better luck next time."

"Next time I'm going to play ping-pong at the YMCA. No dames."

"I was hoping you had a good time. I've got another favor to ask you."

"Ask it, Maguire. Only one thing. Don't try to fix me up with anyone to repay the favor. Better you should be indebted to me than I should get mixed up with another broad like that one."

"I want to see the man who robbed the bank, the one I was asking about last night."

"It's easy. Give me ten minutes to make a phone call or two, then go down to the jail and see him."

"It's not that easy from this end, Wally. No one can know that I'm seeing him. It's important that no one sees me there or knows I'm there. You'll have to arrange to get him out of his cell and take him somewhere private where we can talk."

"You still don't want me to ask any questions about anything?"

"Maybe later, Wally. As a matter of fact, if things go right, maybe I can be of some real help to your outfit there."

"We got J. Edgar Hoover. No reason why we can't use J. Whatever-your-name-is Maguire."

"Patrick," I said, "but only my best friends know that."

"Thanks for the vote of confidence. O.K., I'll arrange it. Make up a pseudonym so I can tell them who's coming. Never mind, I've got the perfect name for you. You can be Mr. Lovelace. J. Edgar Lovelace."

"You mean Lovelace as in Clarice Lovelace?"

"Is she your aunt on your mother's side or your father's side?"

"Look, Wally, the phony name is all right, but there's still one more complication. There's a guy tailing me. He's probably waiting for me outside the building right now. I've got to get out of here without letting him see me."

"This is getting more involved every minute. Seriously, Johnny, don't you think you ought to let me in on this? I can help, maybe. Me and the FBI, we've got a lot of departments and a lot of protection. Tell me what this is all about and I'll figure something out for you."

"The FBI, believe it or not, isn't enough protection for this thing I'm mixed up in. Maybe I'll need you later, but right now, hands off. Promise?"

"You're sure? I mean, I'm mad as hell at you for letting me get involved with that broad last night, but not mad enough to let anything happen to you."

"Nothing is going to happen to me if we play this smart. I've got an idea. Call a hospital, any hospital. Tell them to send an ambulance to One-o-eight South La Salle Street. Tell them a guy has passed out in the men's room on the third floor. J. Edgar Lovelace, that is. Give the superintendent at the hospital the pitch about taking me to the city jail instead of back to the hospital. Tell them to cover me up with a sheet when they take me out of here and keep me covered up when they take me into the jail building."

"With all that excitement, don't you think the guy who's shadowing you is going to get suspicious?"

"If he does, he'll phone his boss instead of following the ambulance. He'll figure the ambulance is going right back to the hospital."

"It sounds very complicated, Johnny. I thought we were the only ones who dreamed up crackpot schemes like this. But if you want me to try it, O. K."

"I'll wait here for your call. Make it fast, will you?"

"I'll call you back just as soon as I've made the arrangements. Hey, you know something? I could get fired for doing this. I'm using the FBI authority for personal reasons."

"If I get killed, you'll get fired. If I come through all right, you may get a promotion. Who can tell?"

While I waited for Wally to phone back, I put my office together again. Danny's boys were slobs but they were thorough, all right. It took me almost half an hour before I got the place looking halfway decent. Forrester didn't call me for three quarters of an hour.

"All clear, Johnny. Get the hell down to the men's room. The ambulance is on the way over."

"What then?"

"It's all arranged. They'll take you right up to a private room. They'll bring the kid up there after you get there."

"Thanks a million, Wally. I know it was a tough assignment."

"Incidentally, Johnny, in case you don't feel so good, those interns on the ambulance aren't going to be any help to you. They're going to be my boys on that ambulance. I don't trust anybody else."

"You're a sweetheart, Wally."

"Sure, from you I get a tumble. From that broad last night I get nothing but trouble. Call me when you get home safe and sound, will you, dear?"

"Ah, you're an ugly mug. But I love you."

I had one break. Nelson's tail wasn't in the upstairs corridor. He must have been waiting downstairs for me. I went down the back stairway and ducked into the men's room on the third floor. It wasn't long before there was some noise outside the door. I heard a man saying, "Now everyone step back and keep clear. I don't want anyone to come in here until we have thoroughly examined this man."

Then a high, squeaky voice said, "But I'm the manager of this building and I have a right to know what's going on."

"You stay out, buddy, until we tell you it's all right. Move back, folks."

Then two men in white interns' uniforms came in quickly, wheeling a very fancy chrome stretcher. One man stayed near the door, leaning against it so that no one could get in. "You the guy?"

I nodded.

"Lie down. Let's get going before we have company. People sure like trouble."

I lay on the cart and they covered me over with a sheet and wheeled me out. There must have been a good crowd in the hall by then. They were making a lot of noise and the thing I heard most often was "Is he dead?" It was hot as hell under that sheet and I was breathing hard. They didn't let me up for air until the ambulance was well on its way toward the city jail. I started to sit up but one of the "interns" pushed me down. "You'd better stay out of sight, buddy. We got orders nobody is supposed to see you until we deliver you to where you're going."

"O.K. to smoke?" I asked.

He nodded.

When we were near the jail they put the sheet over my face again. We got upstairs without a hitch. They wheeled me for a while, I heard a lot of noise of doors opening and closing, then the sheet was lifted back. "O.K., Mister. You wait here. We'll be back for you." They took the stretcher out with them.

The room was small. There were bars on the window and bars on a door in front of a regular door. The room was evidently set up for grilling prisoners. There was a huge spotlight at the ceiling focused on a single hardback chair. At the other end of the room there was a big table with three comfortable chairs around it. I pushed the light button and the spotlight went on and made a big blaze, giving off a lot of heat. I imagined how a guy must feel after he's been under that light and worked over for a couple of hours. I was glad I was on the side of the law I was.

I had made a thorough check for concealed wiring and microphones. There was nothing. I heard the outside door being unlocked and then the iron door. I backed up into a shadowy corner. The prisoner didn't walk into the room. He was pushed. Hard. Hard enough so that he lost his balance and fell to the floor. He made no effort to get up but lay there, motionless, his hands locked together in front of him by handcuffs. The iron door closed. A voice called in gruffly, "There's a button on the wall. When you're through, push it."

The key turned in the lock and then the door was closed and locked. I stood in the corner, trying to get a better look through the half-darkness of the room at the man on the floor. He was a kid, all right. Twenty-three or twenty-four at the most. Tall and thin. I moved closer. Even through the gray prison uniform, you could tell what kind of guy he was. Class came through everything. It was in his face, in the way he combed his hair, and in his build. He was built like the guys you see playing tennis at the fancy country clubs. Or playing polo. I knew the kind.

I walked up and stood over him. His body didn't move but his eyes were big and glassy, staring at me. Fearful. I remembered the girl in the green lace dress. Her eyes had been like that, afire and filled with fear.

"Come on," I said, "let me help you up." I reached out to help him but he wasn't having any. "Come on. I'm not a cop. I came here because I want you to do me a favor." He still wasn't having any. I started to take his handcuffed hands but he pulled them away and rolled over on the bare wooden floor so that his face was against it.

"Look, pal, you've got nothing to be afraid of with me. I told you I'm not a cop. I've got nothing to do with cops. I need help and you're the only one who can help me."

He still wasn't interested. I lighted a cigarette, knelt down, and held it out to him. "Here's a cigarette. Take it. It's good for the nerves."

Slowly he turned over. His eyes were the same, still filled with fear and hatred. I put the cigarette between the lips. He took a long drag and let out the smoke. "Thanks," he said. I smiled. He thought I was a cop and he thought I was out for no good but still he had his manners.

"What the hell do they call a guy named Sanford Wharton the Third for short?"

He sat up, looked at me carefully for a minute, and then got to his feet. He was weak. His face was pale and drawn in at the cheeks. They must have given him the business trying to find out where the money was. But there was a set to his jaw that telegraphed his stubbornness. Nelson and Gloria had picked their man carefully. He wasn't the kind who talked easily.

"My name is Maguire," I said. "John Maguire. I want your help if you can give it to me."

The kid laughed and there was bitterness in that laugh and disillusionment in it and everything else a man feels when he finds out what the world is like, outside his own ivory tower. He did a curious thing then. He let the cigarette fall out of his mouth, squashed it with an angry movement of his foot, went over to the wall, turned on the switch that lighted the tremendous spotlight, and sat in the chair staring up into that huge, hot beam of light. His jaw was set and his hands gripped the arms of the chair. His expression said, I'm ready for anything you want to dish out. I can take it.

I've seen cocky kids, kids with criminal records, swagger around and stick out their chins in defiance of cops. This wasn't like that. This boy walked with dignity and authority. He had command of the situation even though he was handcuffed and a prisoner. The cops would never break him. He was keeping his mouth shut for a reason. He wasn't telling where the money was for a very big reason. It didn't have anything to do with whether he himself lived or died. I could tell right away he didn't care what happened to him. He was clamming up for somebody else or some other reason. It wasn't going to be easy to get him to talk to me. The cops with their hot-box grilling hadn't made it any easier.

"I can see you've been here before," I said. I switched off the light. "Why don't we sit over there? The chairs are better."

"Are you guys changing your tactics?" It was the first time he had spoken more than one word. His voice was deep and had a trace of an Eastern school accent. "I might as well stay here. And you might as well save your time. I've said everything I know. I can't say more than that."

I sat down at the table and lighted a cigarette. "Even so, Wharton, you might as well take advantage of the break. Even if you think I'm a cop, you might as well be comfortable and have a cigarette."

"O.K.," he said, and walked over. I handed him a cigarette and lighted a match for it. He gave me the once-over as he bent forward to the match.

It was a dangerous gamble, but I liked the guy right away and I trusted him. I trusted him to keep his mouth closed. He was no weak sister or a spoiled rich man's son. This man had guts and courage. I figured I'd lay my cards on the table, tell him what I knew. If he wanted to fill in the rest, O.K. If he wouldn't talk, there was nothing I could do. I had to take the chance. I needed information.

"I've got the seventy grand," I said.

He looked at me closely. "They must have brought you in from out of town," he said. "You have a new approach."

"I've got the seventy grand and I don't know what to do with it. I'd like to turn it in to the cops. It would go easier for you if the money turned up. They don't believe that story that you burned it. But I can't turn it in. If I turn it in someone is going to know that I had it and that's going to mean curtains for me."

He kept smiling but didn't say anything.

"I know there's a lot more to this thing than even I know. I'm taking a terrible chance telling you the things I am. For all I know, you're going to turn around and tell the cops. That wouldn't be so bad. But maybe you'll tell Danny Nelson. That *would* be bad. Danny is itching to pull a trigger on me anyway. He'd do it for this. I know he would and you know it."

I watched the guy carefully when I mentioned Nelson's name. There wasn't a flicker. He was a tough one, all right. Hard as nails. "The cops don't know you're hooked up with Nelson, do they? They've got all kinds of theories, but so far they haven't thought of Brother Nelson." He looked around the room. "Don't worry about concealed wires in here. I cased it carefully. You don't have to be afraid to talk."

I waited but he didn't say anything.

"I've got a couple of theories about this, Wharton. I don't know which one is right. Maybe parts of both of them are. I got the dough from Gloria Kirby. She gave it to me because she was scared. She said she stole it from Danny Nelson after you had turned it over to him. That may be true and it may not. The other theory is that Nelson engineered this robbery and somehow Gloria got wind of it and made a deal with you. I've tried to figure this out by myself, but I can't. Also I can't turn around asking questions. The minute Nelson finds out I'm mixed up in this, that is the end of John Maguire."

He moved around in his seat and looked at me once as though he were going to say something, but changed his mind and stayed silent. I was making a little headway, that much I could tell.

"I'm not sure," I said, "just how you and Gloria Kirby are
hooked up. I know her pretty well. A long time ago, before she
was big-time stuff, Gloria and I were—I guess you'd call it in love.
Maybe you're in love with her or think you are. Girls like Gloria
Kirby don't walk into your circle of living very often. They move
in a world all their own. If you fell for her, I can understand it.
I know all about her. In and out of bed." I paused a long time.
"Gloria Kirby is dead." I said it again. "Gloria Kirby is dead." The
iron of his face softened and melted, but not for long.

"Only two people know she's dead. You and me. She was my
protection against Nelson's laying a hand on me. When she disappeared with the dough, Nelson came to me looking for her.
As long as he thinks Gloria is alive, he won't kill me. Maybe
he'll rough me up every day or so, but he won't dare kill me as
long as there is a thread of a chance that I'll lead him to her.
He must not know she's dead, not until I've figured a way to get
myself out of this jam. That's why I've come to you. I need help.I
need the missing details. Maybe, when I know the whole story,
I can get enough evidence to put Nelson in jail and keep him
there, not even let him out on bond long enough to get me. His
boys, too. But I can't risk involving Nelson until my case against
him is airtight." I waited. "Look, Wharton, what you're doing is
your own business. You're not the kind of guy who steals all that
dough for no reason. Your family has dough. I know you're covering up something for somebody. I know whatever you've done
is because you've been pressured or tricked or blackmailed into
it by Nelson. I know how he works. I know how well he works.
That's why I'm scared to death of him. What happens to you is
your own business. If you want to spend the next twenty years in
jail to cover up for somebody else, O.K. But my life is my business. If you can help me out of this jam, it'll make it a lot easier. I
don't want to help you unless you want me to. I'm not even saying
that I can help you. But you can help me get off the hook."

The kid started to talk. "I never heard of Danny Nelson," he said. "I don't know Gloria Kirby, I don't know who she is. I stole the money because I needed it and wanted it. I became frightened with what I had done. I was panicky and I burned the money. That's all I know."

"That much I read in the paper."

The tone of his voice changed. "But suppose—and I say suppose—everything you told me is true. If I am who you think I am, mixed up with these people you've been talking about, how would I know that you aren't connected in some way with this Nelson man, that you aren't here sounding me out to see if I'm going to talk?"

"Are you afraid Nelson sent me? What was your deal with him? It must be that you're protecting someone, keeping your mouth shut to protect someone. Maybe you're taking the rap for all of this to save someone else, and as long as you don't implicate Nelson, that someone else is safe. Is that your deal with Nelson? It makes sense, doesn't it?"

"How would I be sure that you're not an agent for this Nelson man?" he asked.

"There's no real way of knowing, except that Nelson would be crazy to send one of his men to try to see you. First of all, they haven't been allowing any visitors. Secondly, the Chief is after the money. He's got a theory you didn't burn the money but passed it on to some dame. Anyone who comes around here asking for you is going to get a going-over to see how and why he knows you. No, Danny is too smart for that. He wouldn't risk it, wouldn't risk sending one of his men here. He must know you very well. He must know the kind of stuff you're made of, that you don't talk, even under so much pressure. And whatever he's got on you must be pretty important for you to let them send you to the jug for so long without cracking up. If you think it over, you'll see I couldn't be one of Danny's boys."

"Maybe, Maguire. But how did you get in here without going through the mill? Why did the Chief of Police let you by? It seems to me that if what you've been telling me is true, you wouldn't dare risk coming here."

"You're right. It's just as dangerous for anyone to know that I've seen you as it is for Danny. It happens that I've got friends." I told him the story of how I had come into the building.

"I saw the stretcher outside," he said.

"Well, what do you say, Wharton? Can you help me?"

There were many things going through his head. But he was stubborn. Not mean-stubborn, but careful-stubborn, determined. "I can't help you, Maguire."

It was no use. I had laid my cards on the table and he hadn't broken. He had been close once or twice, but not close enough.

"If it means anything to you," he said, "I won't ever talk about what you told me. Remember what I said about not knowing any of these people. I'll stick to that. But just in case you're worried, I'll never mention you to anyone or tell anyone what you've told me."

"Thanks, Wharton. I trust you. I suppose it was a long shot thinking I could get you to talk when no one else could. I took a big risk telling you what I did. But having your word that you won't mention my being here means I haven't lost anything by coming to you. I'm right back where I started." I stood up and started to walk over to ring for the attendant. Thinking back on it now, I don't know why I said it or why I even thought about her at that moment. Before I pressed the button I turned back and said, "You don't know anything about a redheaded doll, do you?"

It hit home right away. I could see it in his face and the way the words landed in his stomach. I put my hand back to my side.

"There are lots of redheaded dolls," he said.

"But there is only one who is looking for Gloria Kirby."

"What about her?"

"The reason I ask is because she's getting herself mixed up in this. I don't know whether she's working for Danny Nelson or against him. She came to me for help—the same way I came to you. I couldn't help her because I couldn't trust her. I wasn't sure whether she was working for Danny or not. I'd hate to see the kid get in real trouble if she's on the up-and-up the way she says."

"Help her, Maguire."

"Yeah?"

"Tell her for me to get out of town. Go back home. Tell her she can't help me. I don't want her to help me. No one can help me."

"She's pretty important to you, huh?"

He lowered his head. "She's my sister."

Then I saw the resemblance. The eyes. Both of them had those green eyes. The color of their hair was different, but there were some expressions that were the same. "I wish I had known last night, Wharton."

"Don't let anyone touch her, harm her in any way. Please."

"All right. I'll do everything I can. You have my word on it. Do you know where I can find her?"

"No. I have no idea. Her name is Marie, but if she's here she won't be using her own name."

"Never mind. I'll find her."

"It's funny," he said, "neither of us can afford to trust each other. Yet we want to very much."

"Whether you help me or not, I'll take care of the redhead," I said. "I don't want that to enter into it. But if there's anything you can tell me, anything at all—"

"I can't, Maguire. I can't tell you one thing without telling you everything. If I told you everything there wouldn't be any purpose left to what I have done. All of this would be for nothing. I'd go to jail anyway and it would be for nothing."

"O.K., Wharton. You know what you're doing."

"Don't let her get mixed up with *him*," he said. "I'd rather see her dead than have him touch her."

I pressed the button. "I'll do everything I can." I walked over to him. "Look, I'm older than you. Not a hell of a lot, maybe, but

I've been through more. You get wised up coming from the side of the tracks I do. You get wised up fighting a war and fighting your way through schools. Maybe whatever this is isn't as important as you think it is. They're going to slam the book at you, Wharton. They'll send you away for as long as they can. Are you sure whatever this is is worth it?"

"I'm sure."

"It hasn't been distorted in your mind so that it's out of proportion?"

"No," he said. "I know what I'm doing."

"O.K., Wharton. Good luck."

I heard the key in the outside door and backed up into the shadows again. The door opened and the light from the corridor streamed in. I hadn't realized how dark it had become in the room. Wharton smiled at me. Then as the iron door opened, his face went back to being stone-like and he walked out of the small box of a room.

He was quite a guy, Mr. Sanford Wharton III. I remember thinking how the wrong guys land in jail.

The two interns showed up in a few minutes and something was wrong. "The Chief of Police is causing a stink downstairs because you got in to see this guy," one of them said. "We've got to move fast. Change clothes with me quickly."

I didn't ask any questions. I started peeling off my clothes.

The taller of the two men was getting his white uniform off. "Just in case there's any trouble on our way out, I think they'd better hold me for questioning instead of you. Make sure you take any identification out of your pockets."

"Good thinking," I said.

"Mister, this is my business. You must be just an amateur."

The man in my suit lay on the stretcher and we covered him up with the sheet. "I'll get your suit back to you," he said. "You can keep the Dr. Kildare outfit as a souvenir."

"Thanks."

Everything was all right until we got off the elevator on the ground floor. Then I heard the loud, profane voice of the Chief of Police. He was really boiling mad. Like a good Irishman, his face was lobster red and his arms were flying through the air like a propeller. We kept the cart moving toward the ambulance backed upto the door. But the Chief stopped us and yelled, "I don't care who said what about anything. I'm running this goddamn show and this man is under arrest." He pulled the sheet back, and I've got to hand it to the FBI man. He was playing the part right up to the hilt. He looked scared as hell. "This man isn't sick. Why the hell isn't he walking? What's going on around here? How the hell does anyone think I can get anything done around here if people keep pulling things behind my back? There's going to be a shake-up around here. A big goddamn shake-up. Not from the Mayor's office this time, but from me. Personally, I'm going to see that everyone who had anything to do with this is going to be hoofing a beat in Cicero. You understand?"

Nobody said anything. The Chief pulled the man off the stretcher and started dragging him down the hall. The other FBI man motioned to me, and quietly we wheeled the cart out the door and into the ambulance. The Chief was so mad he didn't see us go. Even outside we could still hear him blowing his top.

I wiped the perspiration off my forehead. "That was close," I said.

"Wait'll the Chief finds out he's got the wrong guy." He laughed. "I remember once when I first..."

The man's voice droned on and on. I didn't even listen. I was trying to figure out where to start looking for the redhead. And no matter how hard I tried to come up with something else, I always came up with the same answer.

To find the redhead I had to stick close to Danny Nelson.

CHAPTER EIGHT

I took a deep breath, straightened my tie, and then rang the bell. George, Nelson's big boy, opened the door and showed his yellow teeth. "What do you know?" he said.

"Tell your boss I want to see him, Shorty."

"He's going to like that just fine. Just fine." Then, without taking his eyes off me, he called out, "Danny, that Maguire wise guy is out here."

"Send him in, George."

George made a mock bow and I brushed past him in the best tough-guy tradition. I wasn't feeling so tough, I can tell you that. For one thing, I wasn't carrying a gun. I was trying to make this look like a casual call, just dropping in to say hello and see what was new. I can take care of myself, all right. Except when there are more than two guys.

Danny's apartment was everything you could picture a successful gangster's place to be. It was all very modern; big, comfortable, sexy-looking furniture. It was an upstairs-downstairs apartment with a fancy Lucite staircase. There was a big picture window overlooking the lake. It was the same view I had got from the window of Gloria's hotel room.

Danny was sitting at a small table in front of this big window having his breakfast. The newspaper was propped up in front of him. "Hello, Johnny. Glad to see you. You saved me and the boys a trip."

I swaggered over to the table and sat across from Nelson. There was a plate with a few pieces of toast on it. I picked up a piece and started munching it. "You've found Gloria, then?"

"No, Johnny. I didn't find Gloria." He pushed a container of jelly toward me. "It's good jelly. Homemade. My mother made it."

"Funny," I said, "you don't think of guys like you as having mothers."

He laughed. "I guess you're right. Guys like me only have dolls. Like Gloria, huh?"

"No sign of her yet?"

"Not a thing, Johnny. That's why I was going to come around to see you. I thought maybe you'd heard from her since I saw you yesterday."

I shook my head.

"Well, Johnny, she'll turn up. Like I said, she needs that needle so bad she can't last long without it. By the way, Johnny, speaking of needles, have you seen the paper?"

"Yeah. About the guy that was knocked off at the country club last night? I was there when it happened."

"You must have seen an earlier edition. I get the later morning edition, the one with racing news in it. Interesting story." He handed me the newspaper. "Here, take a look."

All of a sudden that newspaper was hot, too hot to handle. It took everything I had to hold onto it without shaking.

LINK HOTEL SUICIDE TO DOPE RING
POLICE SEEK CONNECTION TO
COUNTRY CLUB SLAYING

They hadn't missed a trick. It was the same paper that had made a splash about Vic's murder, bringing up the evils of dope peddling in the city. Now Gloria's suicide was not just a suicide of a woman in a hotel room. They had found the marks of injections in her arm and some wise reporter had put two and two together and it was making for a big story, a lot of big stories. I took my time reading it, stalling for time mostly. Nelson would follow all the way through on the mystery of the unidentified woman who had killed herself because she was a drug addict.

Finally I said, "You think it could be Gloria?"

"I don't know, Johnny. What do you think?"

I referred back to the newspaper. "It says the woman had dark hair and was about thirty-five. That description doesn't fit Gloria."

"That's what I thought. But you know what I thought after that? I thought a woman can change the color of her hair and maybe a doc can be wrong about how old a corpse is. It's hard with people. With a tree you can count the rings around the trunk. Gloria didn't look so good until she got herself all fixed up, her face powdered and all that. Maybe that's why they thought she was older, because she didn't have herself fixed up."

It was a futile try but I made it anyway. "I don't think it's Gloria. Gloria isn't the type. She likes living too well. She has too much to live for."

"But it's like I said about the dope, Maguire. You've never seen one of those people when they come begging for a shot. Their whole personality changes. They do things to get hold of the stuff that they'd never think of doing otherwise. It's funny stuff. It makes people do funny things."

"I hope it isn't Gloria, Danny. For your sake. I know how you feel about her."

"Listen, Johnny, you've got to be realistic at a time like this. If it is Gloria, what am I going to do? I can't stop living." His eyes shifted to the right and a smile broke out on his face. I looked over, too.

She was standing at the head of the Lucite staircase looking like a million bucks. She was wrapped in a long white silk robe. Her hair was combed out long and full so that the redness of it hung over the white of the robe. Right away I thought the worst, that she was a stooge for Nelson. To myself, I called her every dirty name in the book. No words were low enough for her. Yet at the same time my eyes were telling me how beautiful she was and my insides were grinding and telling me how much I wanted her.

Nelson jumped up and waited for her at the foot of the stairs. She was really turning on the charm for him, giving it to him with every dramatic footstep. His face was lit up like a poor kid looking at a rich man's Christmas tree.

When she was down in the room, she wheeled around so that the white robe swirled around her. She hadn't seen me yet. She had eyes only for Nelson. "Do I look all right? It fits me almost perfectly," she said. "It's so lovely." She stroked her hands over the white silk.

"It never looked so good before," Danny said. "Never."

"I don't know how I can ever repay you for being so nice to me, Mr. Nelson. I don't know what I would have done if you hadn't taken me in and taken care of me."

"Not Mr. Nelson, kid. Danny."

This girl was something sensational. She was playing a "poor little me" act and playing it for all it was worth. She lowered her eyes and looked up at Nelson through those thick lashes. "All right, Danny. It's so easy to call you Danny. It's so easy to trust someone who has been as nice to me as you have been."

This was a lot for me to stomach, this line and act of hers. But I stayed quiet and tried not to attract any attention. I wanted to hear as much as I could. It was all so mixed up. She was being so many things. The kid in jail had said to take care of her, not to let Danny lay a hand on her. I didn't know if it was too late for that or not. But she was asking for it. In a way, her modeling of the robe was as bold an invitation to seduction as Gloria ripping off her dress.

"How about something to eat, kid? You had a long trip."

"All right, Danny. I *am* hungry." She took his hand and they started back toward me. When she saw me her face went white and there was an instant when she was unsteady on her feet. Danny had forgotten that I was there. "I forgot about you, Maguire."

"I don't blame you, Danny. If I had something like that walking down my stairs, I could forget everything."

"Get lost for a while, Maguire." He called over to big George, "Take Maguire into the kitchen and tell him a story."

"Never mind, Danny. I just dropped in for a minute. I've got an appointment downtown." I picked up my hat. "Let me know if there's anything new with Gloria." Without waiting for an answer, I started for the door. George blocked my way. Jesus, he was big. I remembered how Humphrey Bogart acts in a spot like this: He sets his jaw and brushes past the strong man. I took a deep breath, moved forward, and ran into a stone wall—and I'm a hell of a lot bigger than Humphrey Bogart. "Nelson, tell your stooge here to get out of my way, will you?"

"Stick around, Maguire. We got unfinished business. You ain't got nothing so important to do. Stick around. We're going out later, the three of us. You and George and me. We're going down to the morgue to look at a stiff."

"I tell you I've got an appointment, Nelson." I walked right up to him. The redhead was watching everything, her eyes wide. "Listen, I came up here out of choice. I came up here because I wanted to find out about Gloria. You can't pull this strong-arm stuff to keep me here. I'm not in this league, remember?"

"Take it easy, Johnny. I'm asking you to stick around as a favor to me. I may need your help down at the morgue."

"If you want my help for anything, you can call me. Right now, I don't have any time to waste." I pretended to say it to Danny but I gave the redhead a look to indicate the information was for her. "You know where my office is, Nelson. If you want me, come up there or call me there. My number is in the phone book." While I looked at the girl, her eyes telegraphed danger and I stepped aside just in time to miss the powerful blow of the blackjack in George's hand. The big man fell off balance. I started running. I got out the front door of the apartment, but the outside entryway was a trap. There was only one door, and that was to the elevator. I looked at the indicator. The car was on the first floor and it was a long way up to the twenty-first floor. I was caught, trapped, and there was nothing to do about it.

I turned around and faced the approaching George. He was smiling his smile of yellow teeth and the blackjack was raised in his right hand. I could have gone quietly and sat in the kitchen, but I was mad as hell. I knew even if I beat the guts out of the guy it wouldn't do any good. Danny and his gun would still be there. But I didn't care. As the thug came nearer I backed up a little, and suddenly shifted, lunged forward, and bucked him in the stomach with my hard Irish noggin. The blow and the surprise caught him and I was able to get the blackjack away from him.

"O.K., big guy," I said. "Try it with your bare fists. See how tough you are."

He was tough. He was plenty tough. As we began going at each other, Danny came out smiling and closed the door to the apartment. We were locked in this room, which was only about six by six. George landed a good one almost right away and I bounced from wall to wall like a billiard ball. The big guy laughed. I shook my head clear and went at him.

Sometime during the fight I rang for the elevator, and in the next couple of minutes I watched the indicator moving up to the twenty-first floor. I began to box then, not just slug. I tried to maneuver George into position so that when the elevator door opened, I could let him have a solid one and knock him into the thing.

When I heard the automatic door open I let him have one in the belly and I put everything I had behind it. It hit him pretty good and he staggered back into the empty cab. But the damn timing on the automatic control was slow and that door didn't close quick enough. He recovered and grabbed me and pulled me in with him just as the door was closing.

Now our arena was even smaller and the damn elevator rocked back and forth on the cables as we went at each other. Somewhere on the way down the car stopped, the door opened. A woman screamed and the scream lasted until the automatic doors closed again. All the way down it was the same. We were both giving out plenty and taking a lot of punishment.

On the main floor the doors opened again. There were people standing there and they began making a hell of a racket. George landed a tremendous wallop to my middle. It knocked the remaining wind out of me. I fell back out of the elevator and onto the cold marble floor of the lobby. George stood motionless for a minute in the elevator, breathing heavily, his shoulders hunched forward like a gorilla's.

That second, the second he stood there, saved me. It was time enough for the automatic doors to close again before he could get out. He pounded on those doors with all his might and I listened as the sounds of the pounding diminished as the elevator went higher and higher.

I was on the edge of passing out. It took everything I had to hold onto consciousness. I pressed the palm of my hand against the inflamed areas on my face, then looked to see if there was any sign of blood. There wasn't. Gradually I moved around until I was able to sit up. I shook the fuzz out of my head and looked at the floor indicator over the elevator door. It had reached the top and was coming down. Time was short.

Everyone in the lobby was talking at once. I didn't stand around to listen to what they were saying. I took off and beat it the hell out of there.

I caught a squint of my face in the rear-view mirror of my car. It wasn't good. Right at that moment I wasn't feeling anything except anger, but I knew later how I would feel, how my body would ache and hurt. I knew how my forehead would want a cool hand on it, except that no hand would be cool enough for the hot hatred in my blood.

Instead of going directly to the office, I went back to my apartment, bolted myself in, got my gun out of the drawer, and made sure it was ready for action. Without letting myself look into any mirror, I went into the bathroom and let the tub fill up. I lay in the heat of the water for a long time, trying to figure this thing out, figure out where the redhead fitted into the picture.

It could have been a phony story about her being the kid's sister. Maybe she was his girl and maybe she was double-crossing him. Yet there had been a sincerity in the guy's eyes. I trusted him instantly. Without knowing anything about anything, I had felt a comradeship with him, felt that deep beat of understanding that there sometimes is between two men. That kind of instinct seldom betrays me. I had depended upon it before to save my life. I had to depend on it again.

If what he had said was true, if this girl was his sister, whatever she was doing at Danny's apartment was for her brother. Somehow, in some way, she was trying to help him. She was doing it the hard way. Giving herself to Danny like that may have been the only way, but it sure as hell was the hard way. I didn't know the timetable. I wasn't sure if she had shown up at Danny's that morning or had gone to him the night before. One thing I knew: Once Danny got hold of her, he would ruin her for any other man and he would ruin any other man for her. It was a stupid thing to be thinking about when my life was touch-and-go at that point. But I wanted her. I knew that with the same blind, dumb instinct of mine. I wanted her and I didn't want her ruined. I didn't want what was left when Nelson was through with her. I wanted her the way she had been the night before, the fleeting vision of green lace in the darkness.

I dried myself carefully. My body was bruised and had begun to ache. I knew that at some time this whole thing was going to fit together, the true story would come together like pieces of a puzzle.

The thing was, was I going to be around long enough to see it happen?

CHAPTER NINE

B ack at the office, I took two aspirins and waited for something to happen. Tina called to ask a couple of questions
about a report she was typing for me. I cut her off short. It was a
good thing, because almost as soon as I hung up the phone rang
again and it was the redhead.

"You got away all right?"

"Sure," I said. "I always get away. Where are they now?"

"They went someplace in a hurry. Maybe to get you. You'd
better hide."

"Listen, Red, I've got to talk to you. Right away."

"It's too dangerous. I just called to warn you. Get out of this,
Maguire. Danny's mad. He'll get you, you know he will. Get away
while you can."

"And leave you in the lurch?"

Her voice softened. "You believe me, then?"

"Baby, I've got to believe you. There's no choice. There's no
other way out."

"Then go away and let me do this in my own way. I can do it.
I think Danny likes me."

"Likes you?" I laughed out loud. "What the hell do you think
he's made of? Sure he likes you. He'll like you until he's used you
all up and there won't be anything left of you that you can call
yourself."

"Let me handle it my way," she said.

"I've got to see you right away."

"I can't. It's too dangerous. Danny can't ever suspect that I know you."

"I don't know what you've got in mind, Red, but you can't do it. You can't throw yourself away to Danny for someone whom you might not be able to save."

"What are you talking about?"

"Your brother. I've seen him."

Her voice almost screamed the words. "When? How is he? What are they doing to him?"

"Easy, baby. He's all right. I made a promise to him. I promised him that I'd look after you. I promised him that I wouldn't let Danny lay a hand on you." I took a deep breath and my hand closed into a fist around the telephone. "Am I too late?"

"Too late?" She had begun to cry. "In a way you are," she said.

"What do you mean, in a way? Tell me, did he or didn't he?"

"He hasn't touched me yet. But it's the only way I can help Sandy. I know it."

"Don't you understand, baby, that he doesn't want your help if it's going to cost you that? He'd rather die than let Nelson get you. Look at it his way."

"I know what I'm doing."

"You think you do, Red. But you don't. You don't know Nelson. You don't know his—well, his habits and his make-up. Look what he did to Gloria Kirby."

"Is she the woman in the morgue?"

"Yes, she could have helped me." the girl said. "She knew the whole story and she could have helped me. Now there's no other way."

"I won't let you. I made a promise to a kid getting kicked around in jail. It's the only thing left to give him courage. I won't let that promise be broken."

"You're wasting time, Maguire. They're on their way to get you right now. This minute."

"I've got to see you, Red, and it's got to be now. Right away. If you don't promise to meet me, I'll throw this whole damn thing into the hands of the police. It'll cost me a lot to do that. Maybe you, too. And maybe it will spoil everything for your brother. But I won't let Danny do it to you. I won't let him do it to you if there is anything in the world I can do to prevent it."

"Don't be a fool, Maguire. Stay out of this. Don't make a martyr out of yourself for nothing."

"It won't be for nothing, Red. You see, I want you as much as Danny does. I don't want what's left after Danny gets through. I want you as you are right now." I waited for her to say something but she didn't answer. "How about it, Red? Will you meet me?"

Softly and after a moment she said, "Where?"

I thought for a minute. I remembered all the clandestine places I had taken women. But this wasn't like that. This girl was not a girl you take to a second-rate hotel. I looked out the window and the sun was shining and the day was warm and bright. "Are you alone in the apartment?"

"Yes. They all went out. Danny told me to rest up, that we were going out on the town tonight."

"Have you got any dough with you?"

"Yes, a little."

"Get out of that building and walk at least three or four blocks. Then pick up a cab and tell the driver to take you out to Fifteenth and Champlain. Southwest corner. It's a church. It's the only really safe place I can think of to meet you. I'll wait for you there."

"And if you don't get there?"

"I'll get there," I said. "And Red?"

"What?"

"You're a hell of a girl. You know that, don't you?"

There was no sound from her. I heard the click as she put the receiver on the hook. You're a hell of a girl, I was thinking. And my mouth was moist with the wanting of her; there was sweat across my forehead and on the palms of my hands. There were all the symptoms and symbols of the approach of love. And these had come without touching her. This had been building up in my mind and gathering speed and gaining substance since the night before. And it was as strong and as bursting as if there had been hours of being alone together, hours of whispering words, soft kisses and hard kisses, the feel of her under my fingers, the sensation of her touch against my body. This welling up inside me was as powerful as that and I had yet to put my mouth over hers.

I put on my hat and went to church.

It was cool there, dark and empty and soundless with the deep sound of a silent church. It had been a long time. Not since I was a kid. This was the old neighborhood. This was the church to which I had gone until I was big enough to say no to my old man and tough enough to defy the passive power of my mother. I was seeing it now for the first time, looking at the architecture, the decaying places in it, seeing the beauty of it and feeling some of the things that are to be felt in a church.

I was thinking, You're getting old, Maguire. Old and soft in the head. When you want a girl, take her to a hotel, not to a church. When your life is in danger, use your gun and use your cunning. Don't pray. But in a way I was praying. I was praying and there was the feel of my gun in its holster against my chest. There were all these feelings, soft and hard. I was going to meet a girl and it was a question of life and death. But I was going to be talking about love. I wouldn't be able to help it.

Alone and waiting for her, I still thought about love, about Gloria and the way she had been and what Danny had done to her. Gloria had come back to me, come back to our love to be saved by our love. It was too late. It had to end the way it ended. But I was having a second chance to have love and to keep that love intact and unspoiled.

O.K., so it was nuts to be thinking about love when maybe my hours were numbered. It was nuts to think I was in love with a girl I had seen only twice and knew nothing about. Maybe. But there was that excitement inside me saying it was love. It was enough. It was more than I had felt in a long, long time.

I waited for twenty minutes before she came. She slid beside me without a sound and took my hand. In the simplicity of that gesture, I came to know that this feeling that had built up inside me was not mine alone. It was matched and made stronger by what she was feeling. By touching hands in the empty silence of the church, we knew each other and we knew each other's thinking and wanting. There was no need for words.

After a few minutes and without letting go of her hand, I stood up and led her toward the front of the church. We paused for a moment at the altar, then walked through an archway behind it. The corridor was lighted by the brightness of the day. We walked to the end of it and through the door leading to the grounds of the church, still without speaking. The bright sunlight turned the wonderful red of her hair to flame as we walked slowly along the walk behind the church.

The caretaker still left the door of his shed unlocked. It opened inward with a faint squeak, and then we were inside, in the cool, quiet dimness of the shed I had known well many years before. But as I looked around, still holding Marie's hand, I saw that the shed was different now, and I was glad. The small window was still coated with dust, but inside the place was clean and neat. The rickety old cot was gone, and in its place was a comfortable studio couch, its cover worn but clean. The battered crates were gone, too, and the caretaker's equipment was carefully stowed on painted shelves against the far wall, instead of lying all over the floor the way it had been when I was a kid.

It took me a moment to realize that there must be a new caretaker here now, just as it was a new John Maguire that came here in search of love. I felt no shame for bringing Marie to this place. In a way, it was a fulfillment. Once I had come here furtively, groping clumsily for something that I only dimly understood,

something that would complete me as a human being and without which life had no meaning. Now I knew what it was that I
had sought then and had been seeking ever since. I held it by the
hand. I turned to look at her.

"Johnny," she began, but I wouldn't let any more words come
out. I thought of many things as I kissed her. I was remembering the other girls I had kissed here when I was a kid, inept and
eager, frightened and cocky all at once. But this wasn't like that.
This kiss was kissed with the sureness of love and the complete-
ness of love and it knew no fright and it knew no false courage. It
knew only that we wanted each other and that our lives could not
continue until we were made one with each other.

In a way it was like getting married. It was solemn, yet there
was no sadness. It was love and it was more than physical love, for
it welled from deep inside each of us, coming together now and
meeting in our mouths, flowing back and forth in that contact.

When it was over, we stood apart, smiling and looking at
each other. There was no question of what was going to happen.
She wanted it as much as I did, and I knew it meant for her what
it meant for me.

She took off her clothes and there was no shame or self-
consciousness in any gesture. I undressed quickly. She saw
the bruises marking my body. The terror returned to her face.
"Johnny, what did he do to you?"

"Never mind, baby."

She touched a blackened area on my side. The tips of her fingers were cool and the touch of her lips against my body was even
cooler. My eyes closed and there was nothing but the delicate
touching of her lips on the bruises on my body. One by one she
touched them, slowly, her lips lingering. I didn't move. I didn't
want anything to spoil what I was feeling. When her lips were
near my ear she whispered, "Do they hurt so much now?"

I tried to speak but no words would come out, only a rough
sound made tight and harsh by wanting.

"Open your eyes, Johnny. Open them, please."

I did.

"This isn't just—"

I cut off her words. "You don't have to say anything. I know what it is. I know what it means."

I pulled her into my arms, and together we sank to the couch. We loved each other and we loved as though we had all the time in the world to be loving. Every part of me came alive to love her. It was not mechanical and surface-satisfying, the way love is with a woman you do not love. It was a kind of love I had never known. I had it now and I held it tightly, thrusting myself forward into the center of love.

Later, when the great physical surge of power had been expended and exhausted, there was time for words and there was need for talking.

"Look," I said. "There's a lot we have to say to eachother. We have a lot of catching up to do, things about you I want to know and things about me that you want to know. Private things. Little things that have nothing to do with Danny Nelson or Gloria Kirby or your brother. But right now we've got to talk straight about these people or there won't be any need to talk about the other things, about you and me. If we don't play this right we're both liable to wind up on a slab in the morgue."

"It doesn't seem fair, does it? For years you look for something." Her hand touched my arm. "I was looking for you, I guess. Now, when it's happened at last, there's this other thing, the trouble Sandy is in. But it doesn't spoil what happened between us. Nothing can ever spoil that." She lowered her head. "It was the first time for me," she said.

"I know. With a man it's different. A man has to—"

She stopped me. "I know, Johnny. You don't have to explain."

"There's nothing to explain. I feel the way you do. I love you."

She was crying and smiling all at once. "Wouldn't it be wonderful," she said, "if we could block out everything, all these horrible things and horrible people closing in on us? Wouldn't it be wonderful if we could escape and forget, never remember anything except that we met and fell in love and we are in love?"

"Gloria Kirby tried that. She wanted to run away and forget and be free of it. She wound up dead. That can't happen to us. I won't let it."

"That's why you won't be able to help me, Johnny. I've got to go ahead and do this thing the way I've planned. I've got to go back to Danny Nelson and let him do as he wants with me until I can get Sandy free."

I stood up. Sitting next to her, our bodies touching, was too much. It left me no room to think. I could be aware only of her. And I had to think. I had to be able to see clearly. I kept my back to her as I put on my clothes. "Start at the beginning and tell me what you know."

"It's so hard to start. Sandy did this for us. That must be it."

"Who's us?"

"My father and mother and me. He must have done it to protect us. This must be Danny Nelson's final way of blackmailing us. It began a long time ago. I didn't know about it until yesterday. Was it only yesterday? My father told me the story when he drove me to the airport, right after we got the call that Sandy had been arrested. It was hard for him. It cost him so much to tell me. He was so ashamed. Up till then it was Dad's secret. His horrible, horrible secret. Now I know it and I think my brother knows it."

"What was the secret?"

"Three years ago. It began when I was away at school. I was in France, studying at the Sorbonne. My father had quite a lot of money. He never was a millionaire, by any means, but he had more than enough. He's a wonderful man, believe that. Everyone loves him, respects him. He does wonderful work for the community. For everyone. It all seems so unbelievable that this could have happened to him. He's the last man in the world you'd think would get in a mess like this. My mother still doesn't know. She must never know. That must be why Sandy is doing this. It's for Mother mostly, so she'll never find out. It would kill her. Really, it would."

"Make sense, Red. We're racing against time."

"Three years ago when Dad went to New York on business, he met Gloria Kirby. She and Danny Nelson had engineered this whole thing. They set a trap for Dad. They knew all about him, how much money he had and how he couldn't risk scandal. Scandal would ruin him, ruin Mother. It would kill her."

"How did they get him?"

"I still can't believe it, Johnny. I really can't. You couldn't believe it either if you knew Dad. He's not like that."

"Where Gloria Kirby was concerned, most men were pretty much alike. What happened, did he fall for her?"

"Yes, I guess so. She must have drugged him or something. It was so cheap, the whole thing. Like a story you read in a cheap magazine." Her voice was down. "Give me a cigarette, Johnny."

I lighted one, handed it to her, then lit one for myself.

"You should have seen him, Johnny, while he was telling me all this. Everything about him came apart. He was older, an old man suddenly."

"Was it the usual pitch? The hotel room and the concealed camera? Picture of your father and Gloria in bed together?"

The girl nodded. "It was more than that. Dad said it went on almost a week before he realized what was happening. Something came over him when he found out. He tried to kill her. They have pictures of that, too, pictures of Dad trying to kill her. Danny Nelson has pictures of everything." She began to cry, shaking her head. "I just can't understand. I can't understand how Dad could have done anything like that. If it were anyone else ..."

"Look at me, Red."

Slowly she raised her head and looked up. She tried to smile. "You wanted me to make love to you before, didn't you?"

"Yes, but ..."

"Just listen," I said. "You wanted me and I wanted you. I wanted you so bad I would have burst inside if I couldn't have had you."

"But Dad wasn't like that. We're young and we're in—in love. It's different with us. It means something with us."

"You never knew Gloria Kirby, you never saw her. I did. I knew Gloria, and there was a time when I was in love with her. She was a hell of a girl, Red. In every way. She was fun and she was exciting. She was beautiful. She was sensational in bed and you knew it about her the first time you saw her. I think inside that I'm a good guy, Red. I'm honest and clean, and yet I loved Gloria Kirby. I can understand any man wanting her, any man at any age. She was that kind of woman."

She didn't say anything.

"Can you believe that I loved Gloria Kirby?"

"But Johnny, she was so cheap, so common! To be mixed up in a blackmail scheme like this—to do the horrible things she did. How could you?"

"If I had said before that I was a killer, a blackmailer, a swindler, would you have stopped me from making love to you? At that point could you have physically stopped yourself from being loved?"

"It's not fair. It's not a fair comparison."

"But it is a fair comparison. That's the point of what I'm trying to say. Sex is something you can't turn off like a light switch. When it hits you hard like that, nothing can stop it. Nothing. And Gloria hit almost every man that way. She had a quality you can't name. But you can smell it and you can feel it and you can feel it gnaw at you. You'd have to be dead or sick or a fairy not to succumb to it. I felt that way. So did your father. We're both men and we've both got blood in our veins, not water or lavender perfume."

"If she were alive now, Johnny, and what happened with us still had happened, could you resist her now? I mean being in love with me and knowing that I love you, could you say no to her?"

I laughed. "I'd try like hell, Red. Honest to God. I'd try like all hell to keep my hands off her."

"But could you?"

"I'm not sure. It's not the kind of reaction you can predetermine. I know I wouldn't want to, a part of me wouldn't want to. It would depend how strong the other part of me wanted her."

She laughed a little and rubbed her hand against her leg. "I never knew Gloria Kirby and yet I'm terribly jealous of her. Silly, isn't it?"

"You'd better tell me the rest of the story."

"That's all really. That's all Dad told me. Nelson had the pictures and started getting money from Dad. There was nothing else my father could do. He could have gone to the police, but then everyone would have known. My mother would have known. It would have ruined everything, everything Dad has tried to build up."

"So he paid out."

"He kept paying out. Huge sums of money."

"How did your brother get into it?"

"We're not sure, really. I mean Dad didn't know Sandy knew anything about this until the robbery at the bank. Dad is sure that Nelson is connected with it some way. He's convinced Nelson told Sandy the story and is blackmailing him. We're not positive of the details, but it must be something like that. That's why I came here. I've got to find out."

"Do you think you'll find it out by living with Danny?"

"With Gloria Kirby dead, it's the only way, my only chance. As soon as we heard about Sandy I decided to come here to find out why he had done it and to help him if I could. After Dad told me the story about himself and Gloria Kirby, warning me that Nelson might be a part of this, I decided that the only thing I could do was to find Gloria Kirby and try to make her help me.

I didn't think any woman could be so inhuman that if I told her about us, she wouldn't want to help me somehow."

"How did you get to me?"

"I followed Danny Nelson. I trailed him every place he went yesterday."

"But how did you find out Gloria Kirby was missing?"

"Well, when I went to Nelson's apartment building, I asked the doorman if Gloria Kirby lived there, too. He said she lived there but she wasn't home and that something must have happened to her because one of Nelson's men had been questioning him, trying to find out what time she left and whether someone was waiting for her and in which direction she had gone. While I was talking to him, Danny and his men came out. So I followed them."

"Tell me something else. How did you get up to Danny's place this morning? Hey, I forgot to tell you that you looked beautiful in that white thing as you were walking down the staircase."

"It was Gloria Kirby's negligee," she said. "I felt funny wearing it. Danny told me I could have anything I wanted in the room. There are such fabulous things there! Jewels and furs and beautiful clothes."

"I still don't see how you got in with Nelson."

"I pulled a bluff. After last night, after you wouldn't or couldn't help me, I was frantic. I took a chance and went right up to his apartment with a suitcase. I left most of my clothes at the hotel. I just took a few plain things with me. I got to see Danny and told him that I was stranded temporarily, I had nowhere to go. I told him a man named Myron Walker in Hollywood had told me to go to Danny if I was ever in any trouble."

"He fell for that?"

"I guess so. He didn't seem to care. I didn't care either.
I just wanted to get in there "somehow."

"Do you know anybody named Myron Walker?"

"Yes. He's an agent or something. Not really, though. Girls go to him to get acting jobs and they wind up doing something else. A girl I knew told me about him once. She had a terrible time. I thought maybe Danny would know him. It sounded low enough for Danny to be mixed up with it."

"Did Nelson know this guy Walker?"

"He seemed to."

"Didn't he ask you a lot of questions?"

"Yes. I answered them, I made up answers and made up stories. I did everything I could to make him want me to stay."

"Didn't he make a pass?"

She held her head down, not looking at me.

"Did he or didn't he?"

"Yes. I let him start but then I put him off. I told him that I was tired, that I had come by bus and it was a hard trip. I don't know what else I told him, but I managed to convince him to wait until tonight."

"You're a brave girl, Red."

"I'm desperate, Johnny. This thing has ruined my father's life and it's ruining my brother's life, too, unless I can help him."

"It begins to make sense," I said. "When I saw your brother this morning I had a feeling that he was covering up for someone. I figured it was a dame. Now I get it. Nelson figured this was a big opportunity. He probably bled your father of all the big dough he could so then he made a deal with your brother. If your brother delivered the dough to him and kept his mouth shut, your father would get the pictures back and the blackmail would be finally over."

"I guess it must be something like that. I've done nothing but think about this, Johnny, try to figure it out every way. It must be something like that."

"He's got an iron will, that brother of yours. The Chief has been using his de luxe treatment to get him to talk. The Chief doesn't believe he burned the dough. But your brother is not

100

talking and I don't think he will, no matter how much heat they put on him."

"Have they hurt him?"

"Not really. They've tried to scare him into talking. He can take care of himself."

"You see, now, don't you, Johnny, that what I'm doing is the only way?"

"No, I don't. Goddamn it, I don't. What kind of a jerk do you think Nelson is? Do you think you're going to let him crawl in bed beside you and whisper little things in his ear and suddenly he's going to give up those pictures and confess to the police so that your brother can get out of jail? Not on your life. Not for any woman. Nelson is smart, Red. He's a whole lot smarter than you can imagine anyone being. And he's got no heart. You can't have a heart in his business."

"I'll find the pictures and I'll steal them."

I smiled. She was so damn naïve. "Where do you think he keeps them, in an album on the piano? Hell, no. He's got those pictures locked up somewhere plenty safe. You haven't got a chance, Red. Not a chance in the world of getting away with any-thing from Nelson."

"But what can I do? I can't just sit back and let this happen to Sandy. I've got to try to help him. There must be some way."

"Sure, there's an easy way. Let your old man talk. Let him tell what happened to him and Gloria Kirby. Then there wouldn't be any point to your brother's not talking. He could tell them why he did it, that Nelson made him do it, and how Nelson planned the whole thing."

"But Dad can't do that. I told you before it would kill my mother and it would kill Dad, too. The scandal would kill him, the shame and the humiliation would be too much for him."

"Then it's no go. We'll have to figure out somethingelse."

"You don't have to, Johnny. Really you don't. Not just because of me."

"I'll let you in on a little secret. I'm in this thing up to my ears. You know why?" I said it slow and easy. "I've got the money your brother took from the bank, all seventy thousand stinking dollars of it. And you know what else? I tried to help Gloria Kirby escape, get away from Danny. He'd kill me for either one of those things if he knew about them. He's got two things against me, Red. He can't kill me twice, but he's going to make me wish I was dead long before he finally finishes me off."

"But, Johnny, if you have the money, why can't you turn it in to the police? It would be easier for Sandy if the money were returned."

"Do you think I don't know that? Sure it would be easier for him. He could give the money back and tell them he stole it in a moment of insanity. He'd get off light. Maybe he'd get off altogether and sit out a turn in a nut house for a while and then go back home. But what about me? What do you think would happen to me if I suddenly turned up carrying seventy grand? Danny would know everything. He'd know I had helped Gloria Kirby and that I'd made a monkey out of him. I'd be dead before you'd know it. Very dead. Beaten to a pulp and as dead as you can get."

I waited for her to say something. "You wouldn't want that to happen, would you, Red?" She didn't hear me. She was busy thinking.

"Johnny," she said, "if I went to the police and told them that you had the money and I told them how you had got it and why Sandy stole it, it would do the same thing for my brother, get him off with a light sentence, wouldn't it?"

"But it's the way I told you. Nelson would find out that I had had the dough and it would be curtains, the end of a short and happy life for me."

"If I don't do it, you'd know how much I love you. You'd know that I loved you enough so that I'd let my own brother go to prison for almost the rest of his life."

"You're getting me nervous even talking about going to the police. Don't even think about that. We'll figure something else out. There must be a way to let both of us off the hook, your brother and I. There's got to be a way."

"My way is the only way," she said.

"Forget it. I'm not letting Nelson lay a hand on you. Even if it would accomplish everything and Danny would let me alone and talk enough to get your brother off light, even then I wouldn't let you. I'd still say there is another way. There has to be another way."

"What is it?"

"I don't know yet. Give me time to think."

She stood up and began to dress. "Hey," I called, "wait a minute before you do that."

"Not now, Johnny. You've got to think."

"The hell with thinking. Come here."

Slowly she walked over to me. I kissed her for a long time. "You see what I was telling you before?"

"I'm not like that, am I, Johnny? Not like Gloria Kirby. I don't reek sex and make you feel—well, like you said."

"Are you kidding?"

"Let me go now, Johnny." I took my arms away and she finished dressing.

"Where do you think you're going?"

"Back to Danny."

"No, you aren't."

"Johnny, I love you. I love you, I love you. But I can't stand around waiting for you to figure this thing out. It's so pointless. There isn't any other way out except for me to do what I'm doing."

"I won't let you."

"You won't be able to stop me."

"I'm not going to let you do it. That's that, and we won't talk about it anymore."

She was dressed and ready to leave. "I'd better go out first and alone. I can find my way."

I was powerless to stop her. If I had had an idea, a plan, anything to offer as an alternative to her throwing herself at Nelson, I could have stopped her. Her plan was futile, I knew that. She had no plan, really, except to go to bed with Nelson and hope that after that she could learn something, or convince Danny to do something to help her. She didn't know Danny very well.

Yet, if I were emotionally removed from this thing and had to work out a plan to trap Nelson, I knew that having this girl at Danny's place was a terrific break, a tremendous opportunity to nail him, get the goods on him once and for all. But I couldn't be a clearheaded opportunist; because this was a girl I had made love to and wanted to love again. Not when Nelson was through with her; it wouldn't be the same then. I'd keep thinking of Gloria Kirby and what he had done to her. I had to do both things: I had to take advantage of the fact that she was living with Danny and make it pay off, and I had to keep Danny from ruining her in the process.

"Listen, Red. I'll figure something out. Go on back to Danny. Stall him off until late tonight. Make him take you on the town. Tell him you always wanted to go to the Pump Room. Make him take you there for dinner. After that go over to the Chez. Tell him you want to see the show. I'll appear at one or the other place. I'll have this figured out by then. I'm sure to have a definite plan by then."

"Johnny, it's futile. We both know that there is no other way."

"Don't you worry, I'll turn up with the answer. It's a good idea for you to stay close to Danny. It will make it easier. But you've got to promise me one thing."

"What's that?"

"That you won't let him touch you. No matter what, you won't let him have you."

"Good-by, Johnny."

"You haven't promised yet."

"I can't promise. If you can't help me, I've got to do it my way."

I grabbed her in my arms and muttered into that wonderful red hair, "You're not alone in this. You've got me to think about. What happens to you happens to me. Remember that."

"Not yet. It can't be like that yet, Johnny. I want it to be, but not yet. When this is over, if it's ever straightened out, then we can be like that. But not yet. Not until this is over. I won't let myself."

"You're stubborn."

"I can't help it."

"You're hard to handle."

"I won't be later."

"You're being a pigheaded damn fool."

"I can't help myself."

"I love you, Red."

She broke down then and clutched me hard. "Save me, Johnny. Please, please save me. I'm scared. I'm scared of Danny, I'm scared of his touching me. Save me, please."

I ran my lips over the silk of her hair. "Don't worry, Red. Don't worry," I said.

But I was worried as hell.

CHAPTER TEN

went directly to Tina's office. She wasn't there.

"Hi, Phyllis. Where's your boss?"

"I don't know, Johnny. I thought she went up to your office."

"To my office? What for?"

"Didn't you call her a little while ago? I'm sure that's where she said she was going."

"I'll go take a look. See you around, Phyllis."

I heard the voices coming from my office. They were making no attempt to be hush-hush. They had Tina in there and I was in no mood to stand around and be cute. I sailed right in.

Tina was sitting in the chair near the desk, the color gone out of her face, her hair disheveled. The rest of the chairs were filled with Danny Nelson and entourage. Danny himself was sitting at my desk, rocking back and forth in my swivel chair.

"What the hell is this all about?"

Danny's voice was pleasant and calm. He had my letter opener in his hand, motioning with it. "Come on in, Johnny, we're having fun."

I went right over to Tina. "You all right?"

"Bored," she said, giving the boys a very cold look, "but intact."

"What's the idea of this, Danny? What are you doing with her?"

"We've been talking, Johnny. We've been telling your girl-friend here stories about you and a dame named Gloria Kirby. You never told her about Gloria, did you?"

"When I'm ready to play true confession," I said, "I'll play it in my own way and not with an audience." I saw George then. He was on his feet, ready for me. It made me mad as hell. He didn't show any signs of our fight. I hadn't left a mark on his ugly face.

"Get out of my chair, Danny. I'm tired. I want to sit down." I walked right up to him. He didn't move, he just kept smiling at me. I grabbed the lapels of his coat and pulled him to his feet. Immediately his three thugs were behind me. Tina screamed. But nothing happened. Danny walked away and lay down on the couch, his thugs dispersed, and I sat down in my own chair. It was only a minor victory but it made me feel better.

"I'm keeping track," Danny said. "I'm keeping track of all these little things you're doing that don't set so good with me. I'm keeping score. We'll settle up later, huh?"

"Listen, Nelson, I'm trying to be a right guy. I'm interested in what happened to Gloria. I stopped by this morning real friendly-like and you pull this strong-arm routine. Well, I'm through. I don't care what kind of score you keep. Whatever game this is, I'm not playing it. You're playing it alone."

George said, "Let me get him, Danny. Let me get him. He's got it coming to him. Let me give it to him."

Nelson laughed. "You got George mad at you, too, Johnny. I thought you were a nice guy, but I guess I was wrong. All of a sudden nobody likes you."

"I like him," Tina said. "I think he's great."

"Thanks, baby."

"How would you like him with his face pushed in, huh?" Danny asked Tina.

She paid no attention to him. "Who are these guys, Johnny? What do they want?"

"I'm not sure. Whatever it is, I haven't got it."

They've been asking me questions about a girl, this Gloria Kirby. You never told me about her, Johnny. Who is she?"

Good old Tina. She was playing it smart. "Just a girl," I said. "I used to know her a long time ago. She's a friend of Danny's now. I'm small-time stuff for her."

"Was she here, Johnny?" She looked over at Nelson. "He keeps asking me if I've seen her around here. Have you been seeing her again?"

Nelson cut in. "Is your girl the jealous type, Johnny?"

"You're damn right I'm the jealous type. Tell me the truth, Johnny, have you been seeing her again?"

"No, Tina. Cross my heart. I haven't been seeing her again. Nelson's got a crazy idea I know where she is. I don't. I haven't seen her in ten years."

"I've got news for you, Johnny," Nelson said. "I know where she is."

"You found her?"

"Sure we found her. Didn't we, George?"

George gave out with his best ugly smile.

"Well, I'm glad, Danny. Did you hold the needle just out of her reach and make her squirm for it? Did you ask her who she saw and who helped her? Did she tell you that she saw me?"

"You're a bad actor, Johnny. You know as well as I do where Gloria is."

"I do? You give me credit for a hell of a lot. I don't know."

"The morgue, Johnny. Remember what the paper said about the girl in the morgue with needle marks in her arm? She done a pretty good job of changing the way she looks. But when you live with a woman as long as I lived with Gloria Kirby, you get to recognize things about them that never change. You know what I mean."

"I'm sorry she's dead, Danny. She was a nice girl once. I don't know what living with you did to her. She was always so full of life, eager to live. You must have given her a bad time for her to end it this way."

"You're breaking my heart, Maguire. Breaking my heart."

"Well, you've found out where Gloria is. Now, why don't you get out of here and leave me alone?"

Nelson jumped off the couch and walked swiftly to my desk, pounding it hard with his fist. "I don't want no more of this fancy talk. You know what I want. Fork it over and make it fast, or your girl here is going to be treated to a show she ain't never seen."

"What are you talking about?"

"Don't play smart, Maguire. I told you. I know you know where it is. Fork it over. The dough. What did Gloria do with the dough?"

"What dough?"

He kept his narrow eyes glued to me and yelled, "George."

Before I could do anything George was in front of me with a leather strap in his hand. He hit me with it across the face. This time Tina really screamed. I tried to get up but George pushed me down again and the swivel chair squeaked and tipped back. I put my hand to my face. There was blood there. My hand came away hot and sticky.

"Where's the dough, Maguire?"

I looked up at him. My teeth were clenched tight and my jaw was sticking out a mile. I didn't say a word. The strap came across my face again. I ducked and it hit me behind the ear. Tina grabbed for the phone. George saw her and lashed the strap and cut across her hand. The phone fell to the floor. Tina was sobbing.

Enough was enough. I stood up, knowing damn well I was going to get knocked down again. This time Danny got his fist into the act. I let myself fall back in the chair, shifting my weight so that the chair went over backward and I fell to the floor. I rolled over quickly. When I came up my gun was in my hand. They hadn't expected that.

That George was a fool. He tried to go at me with the strap. I shot him in the hand and the leather strap fell to the floor. "Anybody else want to play games?"

Nelson smiled. "You fooled me, Maguire. I didn't think you went for guns. I thought all of this was straight stuff about you being a lawyer and on the right side of the law."

"You know better now, Danny. Get out. All of you. Clear out."

"Why don't you call the police, Johnny? Why don't you call the police and tell them all about the nasty men who tried to beat you up?"

Tina said, "I'll call them, Johnny." She picked up the phone from the floor.

"Never mind, baby. It won't do any good. They can arrest Nelson three times a day and three times a day he'll get himself sprung.

"Tell her the real reason, Johnny," Nelson said. "Tell her you don't want to call the police because you'll have to tell them about the dough. You'll have to tell them you've got the dough. Or maybe I'll tell them."

"I don't know what money you're talking about, Nelson. Right now, I've got the gun and I'm telling you to get out of here. All of you. Fast!"

Nelson was taking his sweet time about moving. "One thing you've got to admit, Johnny," he said. "Gloria was a damn good-looking woman. Attractive. Made you turn around and look at her. Practically every man who saw her stopped and took a good look for himself. Even elevator men in office buildings. Like the guy who runs the elevator in this building. He remembered her right away when I described her. I showed him her picture and he said that was the girl, all right. Said he brought her up to this floor."

"Maybe she was in the building, but she didn't come here."

"Johnny, you disappoint me. You got a gun. A man who holds a gun can be brave. Admit it. Be proud of the fact that you fooled me for as long as you did."

"Get out, Nelson. My stomach can't take much more of this."

"I want that money, Maguire. I want it by tonight. One false step and you're finished. Remember that. Your girlfriend, too.

We'll take our time with her. We'll let you watch. Herman over there likes to give it to women. Real good at it. George don't like it with women as much as he does with men. So when Herman is through with your girl, we'll let George go to work on you."

"You've got me scared stiff, Nelson. I don't know anything about any dough. Now, get out, or this gun is going to get jumpy in my hand."

"All right, boys, let's go. Remember what I said, Maguire. I want it by tonight. I'll stand for no monkey business."

Even after the door closed I kept my gun leveled at the door. Tina ran over to me and threw herself against me, beginning to cry.

"Is your hand all right, Tina?"

"Johnny, it was awful. It was awful."

"Take it easy. It's over now."

"Is it over? Is it? You know it isn't. You know they'll get you."

"No, they won't. Not until they find out where the money is."

"What money?"

"Seventy thousand bucks. That's what they're after. They won't dare put me out of the way until they've found out where the money is."

"Do you know where it is, Johnny?"

"Sure. Sure I know where it is."

"Where?"

I dropped my gun on the desk. "You've got it," I said slowly.

"What did you say, Johnny?"

"I said you've got it. It's in your office. I put it there myself."

Tina passed out. She went limp and collapsed to the floor. I let her lie there. She needed the rest. I went into my bottom drawer for the bottle. That bottle had been getting a hell of a workout.

Out in the hall, I rang for the elevator. When it stopped I checked with the man who ran it. "Those guys who were asking you questions this morning—what did you tell them?"

"What guys, Mr. Maguire?"

"The ones who asked if you saw a blonde come up here yesterday morning."

"Nobody asked me. It must have been Harry."

"Yeah," I said. "It must have been. Go ahead down. I'll ring for the other car." I pressed the button and waited for the other elevator to come up.

"Harry, those men asking you questions this morning—what did you tell them?"

"What men, Mr. Maguire?"

"Wasn't there anyone around here asking you if a blonde had come to see me yesterday morning?"

"No, sir."

"You've been on all morning?"

"Sure. Me and Milt, we've been on since seven this morning. Nobody's asked me nothing. I brought a gang of guys up to this floor. Maybe they were going in to see you."

"O.K., Harry. Go ahead. Thanks."

That Danny Nelson was a smart one, all right. He had pulled a bluff and it had almost worked. I thought back on what I had said. I hadn't cracked. I could have kicked myself for believing his story about checking with the elevator men. It was an old bluff and I had fallen for it. Luckily not hard enough.

When I went back in my office, Tina was sitting up on the floor drinking out of the bottle. "For people who burn mink coats and have seventy thousand dollars lying around, we sure drink cheap liquor," she said.

CHAPTER ELEVEN

"Johnny," she said. "Why can't we take the money and go away together? We could go far away where he would never, never find us. Please, Johnny. Let's do it now. While there's still time. I'm afraid. For the first time, I'm afraid for myself as well as you. Please, Johnny. Please."

"What the hell is this? Everybody wants to go away on that dough. It doesn't belong to me. Can't you understand that? The dough belongs to a bank. It's not for me to run away to Tahiti on."

Tina got up from the floor and lay on the couch. "Is that why she came to you, Johnny? Did Gloria Kirby want to run away with you, too?"

"That was an afterthought."

"What was she like?"

"Gloria? I don't know. A woman. A hell of a woman." What else could I say? How can you tell one woman about another woman, about what another woman does to your insides?

"Were you—were you in love with her?"

"I guess so. A long time ago. Jesus, Tina, I've got a million things on my mind. Do we have to talk about it now?"

Her voice was soft, calm, but underneath there was that hard, tough determination that Tina gets sometimes. "Yes, we have to talk about it now. We'd better talk about a lot of things now."

"I'm not in the mood."

"Aren't you, darling? Well, that's too bad. I am. You're never in the mood to talk about *us*. But you can't keep putting it off indefinitely. What happened before was pretty bad, Johnny.

It was terribly frightening. An experience like that makes you think about many things."

"I'm sorry you had to be dragged into it."

"Don't you see that I'll always be dragged into things with you as long as—well, as long as we're together?"

"Tina, please. Of all the damn-fool times to be talking about us!"

She was mad now. I'd never seen her like this, so full of fire and so full of determination. "You listen to me, John Maguire, and you listen hard. I've had enough of being put off and pushed around. I've been a sap long enough. I love you, Johnny, and it's cost me a lot to love you the way I do. It's cost me my self-respect sometimes. There's been so much heartache and so much humiliation. I'm always Tina, the girl to come back to after you take a fling with someone else. How long do you think I can take this?"

"You've always known how I've felt. I've never tried to hold you back. If you want to shake, shake me. I've told you a million times to get another man, a marrying kind. I'm not like that."

"It's so easy to say, 'Forget about me.' I've tried that. I've tried over and over again. Sure you push me away. But only with one hand, Johnny. With the other hand you hold on to a thread of me. You keep coming back. Just when I think this time you're gone for good, this time you've found someone else and it's for keeps, then suddenly you're there again and you have your arms out to hold me and I can't help myself. I simply can't control myself."

O.K., so I was a heel. It would have been easy at that point to placate Tina if it hadn't been for the redhead. The memory of her was so new and so real. My body still quivered from being with her and my lips still tasted the fluid of her mouth. "All right, I admit it. It's my fault. I shouldn't come back. Ever. It's not fair to you."

"I know how you feel, Johnny. I really think you're sincere when you say that you want me to meet another man and get married. If you didn't keep coming back to me, I could believe it, believe that deep down inside you meant it. But you do come back to me. There must be a reason for it."

"Because I haven't got guts enough, maybe, to be a right guy. I know you're waiting and you're so ..." I hesitated, caught in the trap of my own words.

"So what? So convenient?"

"I didn't mean that. You're—well, you know what you are."

"How long has it been, Johnny, that we've had this—what do you call it?—arrangement?"

"We've known each other four years," I said.

"And in those four years, how many times have you thought that you've been in love? How many times have you wandered off after another woman only to find it meant nothing after all and then come quickly back to me?"

"What's the point of this, Tina? What are you trying to prove?"

"Nothing. Nothing except that I think you love me. You must love me. That's the only reason you keep coming back to me."

I thought about it a long time before I said it. I knew my feelings about Tina, I knew how close I could come to loving her. There were many times I felt I did love her, that what I had with her was real love and these others were just exciting false alarms. But basically I couldn't fool myself. There was a real love somewhere and it was the thing I continually hunted. And I had found it now. Even though everything in the world seemed to be working to keep me from holding onto that love, it made the redhead even more desirable, more worth having.

Tina, in her way, was quite a girl. I knew that very well and I had always known it. She was smart and strong and dependable and sensible. She meant a lot to me. In some ways more than other women possibly could. So I thought a long time before I said it. Then I told her. "This time," I said, "no matter what happens, I know I won't come back."

She sat up. "This time? What is it this time?"

"A girl. It happened, Tina. It's what I've been looking for and waiting for. It's happened to me now."

She was silent for a moment. I was afraid she would begin to cry. But she didn't cry. She laughed. She laughed hard and loud.

"What the hell is so funny?"

"Each time you say, 'This is it.' Your new girl is always it, the final answer, the end of being a lonesome hunter. Do you remember how many times you have felt this way?"

"This is different."

"Is it? Are you sure?"

"I'm very sure."

She stood up. "All right, Johnny. Remember what you said. You said this time, no matter what happens, you won't come back to me."

"You have my word."

"Johnny, tell me something."

"Sure."

"What is it that you keep looking for? What is it that you keep thinking a woman, a special woman, can give to you?"

"I'm no good at words, Tina. You know that. It's just that—well, it's a lot of things. You know it by the way you feel. You can't know it in words or the way people write in a book. It's hard to understand."

"No, it isn't," she said. "Not for me."

"I'm sorry, Tina."

"For what? For me? You certainly can't be sorry for me. You never told me you loved me or that I was it. You never said I was the woman you were looking for. I'm a big girl, Johnny. We've never lied to each other about how things were. My eyes have been wide open. It's always been kicks and laughs for us, strictly for convenience."

"Stop talking, will you? Whatever it was we've had together, leave it alone. It was good and wonderful. Don't try to spoil it by taking it away. Don't make it sound cheap and common. It was never that, never like that, and you know it."

Her stenographer's pad was on the desk. She picked it up. "I don't want to be dramatic, Johnny, but you have a key of mine. I'd like it back."

Suddenly I felt the weight of the keys in my pocket. I didn't want to give it back. The realization of Tina's importance to me came with a rush of blood to my head. The key in my pocket was a gold one she had given me as a present. Her key with my initials. It was important now. Important to hold on to. "Let me keep it, will you, as a kind of souvenir?"

"It would be the beginning of an interesting collection, wouldn't it? 'Keys to the apartments of girls I have known,' you could call it. You could have them mounted on velvet, frame them, and hang them over your fireplace someday when you have a house with a fireplace."

"Stop it, Tina. You know it isn't like that. I'd just like to keep it, that's all."

"No, Counselor, not this time. As long as you have that key, I'll be listening for the sound of it in the door. I don't want to do that anymore."

"You're being silly about this. I told you this isn't the time to talk about it. You're upset. Nelson and his boys are enough to upset anyone."

"Maybe it's what I needed. Maybe I needed something to scare the hell out of me so I could see the way things really are with us, see it clearly." She held out her hand. "Come on, Johnny, it doesn't have enough gold in it to be worth *real* money."

It was a hard thing for me to do. I was remembering the night she had given it to me. The key had been shining and bright. We had laughed about it. I had taken it casually and used it casually. Now it wasn't new and bright any more. The gold had become duller and there were marks and dents from my own keys scratching against it. I was all thumbs trying to get it off the ring. I put it into her waiting hand. I opened my mouth to say something but there was nothing to say.

Tina's hand closed into a fist around the key. "I hope," she said, "that the Legal Stenographic Bureau won't lose a client because of this. You know me, Johnny, I always have an eye for business."

"Won't it make it hard for us? I mean if I have to sit in your office and give you dictation and—You know what I mean."

"There's Phyllis. She's really getting quite efficient and fast."

"Listen, Tina, about this other business with Danny Nelson, don't be frightened. He won't touch you. I'll see to that."

"I'm not worried any more, Johnny. If he's going to torture someone, I'm sure he'll find your true love. I won't be important enough."

"This is such a goddamn mess. If you hadn't insisted on talking now, if you only could have waited until this was over. Neither of us are clearheaded enough to be making decisions now."

She shook her head and smiled. "That's not true. I feel very clearheaded. More clearheaded than I've felt in a long time." At the door she stopped and turned back to give me a long look. "Well, I'll see you around, huh, Counselor?"

"Sure," I said. "See you around."

CHAPTER TWELVE

I needed to see the redhead again. I needed to see her and to hold her and to know that she was real and that this thing that I was feeling for her was alive, as vitally alive as I wanted it to be. There was a tentative void in me, one less key on my key chain. It would be all right if this were really love, I thought. The void would not be a void if this were love. Yet it couldn't be anything else. I wouldn't have been feeling this way if it were anything else but love.

Love, I thought. Love is a pain in the neck.

A thousand times I cursed myself and called myself a fool to become entangled this way with the redhead when the questions were not of love and of loving but of life and living. I mentally kicked myself for letting Tina bring our relationship into such sharp focus, so sharp that it was either everything or nothing at all.

So many things were pressing on my mind, crowding my awareness, breathing danger down my back. I thought that if only I could be holding the redhead now and drawing the security I needed from the touch of her, the breath of her, and the warmth of her mouth, it would be all right. I would know my feet were on the ground and my head was clear and I could face squarely what lay ahead to be faced.

But she was with Danny. Probably now he had gone back to her and this was the preliminary bout, the fencing for position. His head on her shoulder. A sloppy kiss. A playful pat on her rear. The main bout would be later that night. I couldn't stop the picture of it from leaping into my head. I kept seeing them in bed together, Danny's hands on her body, her submission to him. For what?

For what?

For a lot of things. I knew them well.

There was a way out, I told myself. There had to be. I knew if I wasn't so goofed up inside, heart and head all mixed up and ineffectual, I could see the way out. There would be a way to trap Danny, to nail him once and for all. There was a spy in his own house. The redhead was potentially the most effective agent the law could use to lead Danny into a trap.

I sat down at my desk, took out a clean sheet of paper, sharpened my pencil, and faced the blankness of the paper with the point of lead. It was futile and I knew it. I had got out of spots before; I had had flashes of intuition that had given me an idea, a gimmick. They hadn't come like this, not sitting and waiting for them to come. They had come quickly, unexpectedly, and I had known they were right instantly and with a sureness.

Finally I drew a big question mark on the clean paper, pressed the point of the pencil until it broke, crumpled the sheet, and threw it on the floor.

I telephoned Wally Forrester at the FBI.

"Wally, meet me for a drink."

"Gee, Johnny, I've got a deskful of—"

"It's important."

"O.K., pal. Whatever you say."

"Let's make it someplace out of the way. I can't risk being seen with you. There may still be a tail on me. I'm not sure. Got any ideas?"

"There's a saloon on the lower level near the river. Think it's called George and Fred. Something like that. It's like a catacomb down there. Might be a good place, particularly if you want to shake someone."

"Half hour too soon?"

"No, I can make it."

"I'll see you there."

"Johnny?"

"Huh?"

"Think you ought to give me a few hints? I mean in case something happens before we meet."

"Nothing will happen."

"But just in case, Johnny, say something. Anything that'll give me a lead if there's trouble."

"Danny Nelson," I said, and I hung up.

When I went downstairs there was a tail waiting for me, the same guy who had been on the job since the night before. He had smartened up some. From where he waited he could watch both exits of the building.

I made a point of talking to the elevator operator in a loud voice. "There's going to be a guy here to see me in about ten minutes," I said. "I'm going next door for a quick beer. Tell him to wait, will you?"

The shadow followed me until I went into the bar. He anchored himself between my office building and the building the bar was in. I hoped he figured I meant what I said about coming right back. I had a quick beer at the bar then faded toward -the back of the room and out the rear door. Luckily, I cased it first. One of the men who had been in my office with Nelson was out there, walking back and forth. He wasn't making any pretense at staying undercover.

There was a big beer truck up near the door. I waited until the guy's back was turned and I made a running leap and broad jump into the truck, knocking my head on a barrel when I landed.

There were ten perilous minutes as I waited for the truck to get going. After we had been going for a while, I rapped on the window. The driver looked startled, then mad. Finally he stopped and let me out. He started to give me a bad time but I pulled out a ten spot and he changed his mind.

Forrester was sitting at the end of the bar when I came in. I found a dark booth and in a little while he brought his drink over. "You know, Maguire, I'm glad I'm not your mother. If I were your mother I'd worry about you."

"I'm glad you're not my mother, too. I might have inherited your fat can and bowlegs."

O.K., so you got a thing about playing cops and robbers, Johnny. But this time you've got yourself in with a big operator."

"What would it be worth to you to nail him, get him on something so that you can throw the book at him?"

Forrester smiled and took a swallow of his drink. "Better men than I have tried. Nelson is careful. You never can catch him with nothing."

"I asked you what it would be worth to you."

"You mean in terms of dough?"

"No. What would it mean to you personally with the Bureau?"

He shrugged his shoulders and smiled. "They'd tell J. Edgar to get lost. Me, I'd be the hottest boy in the department." Then he looked at me closely. "What would it mean to you?"

"My life, maybe. A girl. A girl I love."

"You, Maguire, in love? This I got to see."

"You're looking at me."

"I'd like to get a look at this girl. You mean real love? Churches and weddings and stuff like that?"

"Listen to me, Wally, and listen carefully. What would happen if one of your agents walked in on Nelson and caught him in the act of shooting dope into someone?"

"We could nail him on a narcotics charge. In Nelson's case we could go a lot farther. Once we had him on something solid, we'd have a right to investigate further. There's a lot of stuff we could turn up on Nelson if we had the opportunity. You see, the law protects a guy like that. Until you catch him doing something, you've got no right to tear apart his apartment, look for stuff, or investigate records. We've tried nailing him on income tax, but that's as clean as a whistle as far as anything we could find."

"I think I can arrange it. Set up the dope business."

"You mean just like you said, right in the act of shooting dope into somebody?"

"Yes."

"Sounds good."

"It's a deal, though. I'm trading this to you for something else."

"Go ahead."

"If it works and you begin finding things, you're going to find that Nelson had a blackmail racket on the side. Photographs. I want the right to go through those photographs and destroy what I want. O.K.?"

"Is he blackmailing you?"

"Hell, no."

"I can promise that. What else?"

"That kid I've been talking to you about, the one in jail. You've got to go to bat for him and get him off. With a light sentence, anyway. He did this because he was blackmailed into it."

"I can't promise anything there, Johnny. I can try. I can promise to try."

"That's good enough for me, Wally."

He signaled the waiter and ordered a couple of drinks. "Let me ask you something, Maguire. How do you figure in this?"

"I can't tell you that. All I can tell you is that it's important to me."

"What's going to happen to you?"

"It's going to be risky. You've got to arrange this thing so that all Nelson's thugs are arrested at the same time, or at least quick enough so they don't have time to get wise to me and knock me off when I'm not looking. You're also going to have to arrange it so none of them get out on bail. As far as I know, there are only three guys that Danny uses as trigger men. I can name them and tell you how to get them."

"You're taking an awful chance, Maguire. I guess maybe we can arrange it so Nelson can't get out of jail. We won't be able to stop him from seeing a lawyer. He can give the word to have you bumped off."

"I'll have to take that chance. If it happens, you might throw the fear of God into the lawyer. Or maybe I'll beat it out of town for a while."

"You know if Danny Nelson wants your hide, he'll get it if he can, no matter where you go."

"My life is like that, Wally. I've been in risky businesses before. All those things through the war and some other things. You know a little bit about it. I can't be scared by anything anymore. I'm reasonably sure that if you get Nelson and his three thugs, I'll be safe."

"O.K., Johnny. Tell me what to do."

Funny thing, the plan came out fast and clear, as if I had been thinking about it for a long time. It took shape as I told it to him.

"It's a hell of a risky plan, Johnny. There are too many things that can go wrong. It depends on almost everything going right."

"If it doesn't work, what have you lost?"

"Me? The Bureau? Nothing. But what about you and this—"

"We're behind the eight ball anyway. It couldn't be any worse."

"It's a long shot, Johnny. The Bureau doesn't play long shots. They wait until the odds are better."

"How long have you waited for Nelson?"

"A long time."

"Have the odds become shorter?"

He shook his head. "Not really."

"I'll make the arrangements and phone you later. You'll be ready?"

"Sure, Johnny, we'll be ready."

"Listen, there's one more thing. Between now and then, there may be some trouble. I can handle myself all right, but there's a girl involved. I'm not sure if they'll try anything with her. In case they do—"

"This is the girl you love?"

I waited a minute. "No, this is another girl. They've threatened me. If I don't talk, they say they'll do something to her."

"Where is she now?"

"At her office. But if you put any of your men on her now, it'll be a tip-off to Nelson."

"Call her up and tell her to go to a movie," Wally said.

"To a movie?"

"Yes. Tell her to go to the Clark Theatre. They're open almost all night. When she gets past the ticket taker, tell her to drop a glove, pick it up, and go in and sit down. Tell her not to leave the seat until she gets the word from us."

"You want her to go right now?"

"Yes."

"It's going to be quite a long sit. I hope it's a good movie."

"They got westerns. Everybody likes westerns."

"You'll have a man there, huh?" Forrester nodded. "What if she's tailed?"

"So what? If they tried to touch her, our men will nab the guy and keep him out of touch with the world until this is over."

"O.K., Wally. Thanks for everything."

"It may be nothing but a lot of trouble for you."

"I've got to take the chance."

"I'll stay at my phone from now on. Keep me posted every hour or so."

"Listen, pal, I know you pretty well and I know you're interested in looking out for me, but if you've got any ideas about putting a bodyguard on my heels, forget it. It's too risky. We can't tip Danny off in any way."

He smiled. "It never crossed my mind."

"Pick up the check, Forrester. If this comes off you'll get a raise and then you can afford it."

He picked it up with a smile. "I can't afford this after last night and your friend Miss Lovelace. Honest to God, Johnny, did you really ever get anything out of that dame?"

"It's all in knowing how, Wally."

"Good luck, Johnny. Don't forget to tell that girl to go to the movies."

I phoned Tina right away. As soon as she heard my voice she said, "Oh, yes, Mr. Sorenson, I'm working on your stuff right now."

"Trouble?"

"Yes."

"Nelson there?"

"No, Mr. Sorenson. Just auxiliary things."

"His thugs?"

"Yes."

"How many?"

"Two."

"Are they looking for me?"

"Yes, Mr. Sorenson, in the worst way."

"Do you think they'll let you out of there?"

"I'm not sure."

"Listen to me, Tina. I'll figure a way to get you out of there and here's what I want you to do. Go to the Clark Theatre. It's right at Madison there. Go in and when you get past the ticket taker, drop your glove, pick it up, and go inside and sit down. You'll be protected. Don't worry. But don't leave that theatre until someone comes to get you. I'll try to do it myself."

Her voice was icy. "You don't have to bother."

"Don't be funny. This is serious. It may be a long sit, but sit it out. Promise me that."

"Very well, Mr. Sorenson."

"I'm not sure how I'll get the boys off your tail, but I'll do it. The minute you can, beat it out of there."

"As soon as I can, I will."

"And don't worry. You'll be all right."

"But will you, Mr. Sorenson?"

"I'm glad to see you haven't become completely heartless about me."

"That's the way I am, Mr. Sorenson. I'm very conscientious. Where my work is concerned, I put my personal feelings entirely aside. I'd feel the same way about anybody."

"Very funny, Miss Weston. Now go ahead and stall for time. You know how. They're not pulling any rough stuff, are they?"

"Not yet, but I think soon."

"I'll work fast. Keep your chin up."

As soon as I was through talking to Tina, I got a dollar's worth of change from the bartender and called up every lawyer in the building I could think of. I gave them all the same line. I told them it was Tina's birthday and to go right down there for a party; I was on my way over with free liquor. I told them to pass the word on. The way those boys headed for a free drink, I knew her office would be loaded with thirsty, anxious people within fifteen minutes.

I had two drinks in twenty minutes, then phoned her back. There was a lot of background noise when she answered the phone.

"How's it going?"

"They've gone. They may be waiting in the hall for me."

"Clever idea, huh?"

"There are going to be a lot of irritated lawyers unless you show up with the hootch. There must be thirty thirsty men here."

"Well, surround yourself with at least six of them and get out of there."

"What if they try to stop me?"

"If you get enough men around you, they won't. Tell those lushes you have a wonderful idea. Tell them you're going out to buy some liquor to keep going until I get there. Ask for six volunteers to accompany you. It's only a couple of blocks to the movie house. You can do it."

"All right. I guess I can."

"Listen, I'm sorry about this. I had no right to get you mixed up in it."

"It's too late for that. I'll do as you say."

"I wish there were something else I could tell you that would help, that would make this easier. I can't right now. But later I'll be able to tell you about it."

"All right, Johnny. And Johnny…"

"What?"

"Take care of yourself."

"Don't worry."

"I wish," she said softly, "that I didn't care enough to worry."

It came off all right. There was an office building across from the Clark Theatre. I was watching out of the third-floor fire escape when Tina and the boys came up to the box office. I'm not sure what she told them, but there was suddenly a big argument among them. In the confusion, Tina bought a ticket and slipped inside.

I didn't see Nelson's men but I was certain that they were close by. I checked my watch. It was a little after five. I put myself in the middle of the crowd leaving the office building and hopped on a crowded streetcar, not caring much where it was going.

CHAPTER THIRTEEN

The street car was going south. I rode it for an hour, packed in with a hundred other people, jostled by them, pushed by them, and stepped on by them. Softly and under my breath I cursed them one by one, these workers riding home. I cursed their abusing me and I cursed them for the way they smelled and for the way they talked and the way they lived. Yet these people were bystanders, guilty of nothing. As I swore at them, I wondered who I should be cursing instead. Gloria? In a way, because she had got me into all this. Still, if it hadn't been for Gloria I would never have met the redhead.

Marie.

Funny, I had never called her by her name. I was cursing her, too. I was thinking that if it weren't for her, if I could be heartless and reveal the story of Nelson's blackmailing, not caring who suffered because of it … If it weren't for her, my relationship with Tina wouldn't have been forced into a showdown. I knew it was selfish of me to cling so stubbornly to Tina when I loved someone else. But there had been others before, and I had thought they were real. Then suddenly those loves had blown up, and when the smoke cleared there was nothing left. Except Tina. Always the same and always loving me. Now, if this love blew up, there would be nothing. Not Tina any more. I felt again the lightness on my key chain, one key missing.

A woman rammed an umbrella into my side as she hurried off the car. This time I swore out loud.

Curse Danny Nelson, I thought, not her. But you don't deliberately curse a man like Nelson. The whole country curses him and curses him constantly, rebels against him constantly. There was nothing to damn Nelson for. When you get mixed up with him, you expect this, you expect the worst.

The person I was really cursing was myself. Me, because I was a fool and I led with my chin and my heart was right behind it and reason was five miles away. I was thinking that when this was over and everything was allright, never would I allow myself to get mixed up in a mess like this.

I knew damn well that if everything was going to be all right it was because I and the FBI were going to make it all right. It would never come by succumbing to indulgent introspection like this. Action was the answer. Action divorced from feeling. Clean, cold, steel-like action, calculated and premeditated.

At the next stop I pushed my way through the crowd and got off the streetcar. It was some God-forsaken neighborhood. I walked until I found a cab, hopped in, and gave the driver Danny Nelson's address. I made him stop a block away, then I walked cautiously toward the big apartment building where Nelson lived. I liked what I was doing. Maybe to a lot of guys it wouldn't make sense, walking directly into the heart of trouble. But if Danny was looking for me, he wouldn't look under his nose. He wouldn't look in the shadows of the alley across the street. I learned that technique from a girl once when she made a hell of a direct pass at me. "The best defense," she explained, "is offense."

They came out in a cluster, the three thugs circling Nelson and the redhead. The big guy, George, had his hand in a sling. I smiled to myself. That made me feel pretty good, too. I patted my gun in its holster. Reassurance.

She was looking good, my girl. Gloria's clothes fitted her well, but hell, I suppose mink looks good on anybody. A big black chauffeur-driven car pulled up. Danny and the redhead got in. The thugs stayed in front of the building, talking to each other. Then they dispersed, each one in a different direction. So far, so good. Marie had got Danny to take her out. First stop was the Pump Room. I checked my watch. There was no hurry. Hell, let them eat.

I walked across the street and talked to the doorman.

"Hey, Mac, you got a public phone in there?"

He shook his head.

"This is awful important. I ran out of gas back the street there and I got to call a garage."

"There's a filling station up a block or two."

"I belong to the Motor Club. They'll come and get me out of trouble and it won't cost anything except for the gas. You sure you haven't got any kind of phone in there I could use?"

He looked me up and down. "O.K. There's a phone near the service elevator." He pointed inside the lobby. "You see that there door?"

"Yeah."

"Go through there and keep going to your left. You can't miss it. Make it snappy, though, will you? They don't like no strangers hanging around here."

I tossed him a quarter. "Much obliged, Mac."

I took my time casing the place. There was a stairway and a back elevator. The rear door was locked with a button latch. I pressed it so that it was unlocked from the outside. Just in case somebody relocked that, I opened the safety lock on two basement windows. I was going to have to get in there later and I wanted to be as quiet as possible.

Then I called Wally Forrester to report in.

"Proceeding as scheduled, Wally. They're on their way to the Pump Room. In two or three hours they'll be at the Chez."

"Where are you?"

"Nelson's apartment building."

"Pretty risky, isn't it?"

"Not a bit. If you were looking for me, would you expect to find me in the lobby of your building?"

"Listen, Johnny, I've been giving this plan a lot of thought. It's not making any sense to me. There are too many holes in this. It depends on your making the arrangements with this girl. How are you going to get to talk to her without Danny knowing about it?"

"I got a plan, Wally. Don't worry about that."

"To be honest with you, Maguire, I *am* worried. I don't think it's going to come off."

"You've got nothing to lose."

"But you do, Johnny. Plenty."

"I'll phone you later, Wally."

He hung up.

The Pump Room gets a very posh crowd. From a poor man's saloon across the street, I looked through the plate-glass window and watched the rich people going in and out. Nelson's car and chauffeur were there. Once, while I was there, the chauffeur came in and had a fast drink. I thought for a minute about striking up a conversation with him, but I figured there wasn't much I could learn from him.

George showed up, went in, and came right out again. In a few minutes Nelson came out and they stood together on the curb talking. George kept shaking his head and shrugging his shoulders. This I took to mean that John Patrick Maguire was among the missing. Nelson became excited, waved his hands in a few directions, and George was on his way.

I reported in to Forrester a couple of times during the long wait. I could tell he was getting tense. He made no chitchat about Clarice Lovelace. I tried to go easy on the drinking. I wanted my head clear. But I couldn't let myself think about what was going to happen. Wally was right, it was a hell of a long shot, it depended on so many things.

At eleven-thirty Nelson and the redhead appeared at the door. He flagged his car. I watched as they pulled away. It was the right direction. They were going to the Chez.

The Chez isn't as swank as the Pump Room. It's what you expect a big night club to be; crowded and gawdy, lots of noise, good show, fabulous people. In the back there's a bar, separated from the main room by a glass window. This is so the cheaper customers can look at the floor show but can't hear anything. A radio broadcast is run from there every night. It was a cute show put on by a husband-and-wife combination. They made small talk about daily living, got phone calls from listeners, and interviewed bar flies or celebrities from outside the glass wall.

Not wanting my phone call to get on a national network, I called the Chez and asked to speak to Mike on a private wire. The headwaiter, who answered the phone, gave me the business about Mike and Buff being on the air, but I was persistent and pretty soon Mike came to the phone.

"Do me a favor, pal, will you?"

"What is it?"

"There's a guy on his way over there. Interview him on the air for a long time. Get him to tell you the story of his life."

"Who is he? We can't put any shmoe on radio."

"The guy's name is Danny Nelson. Mean anything to you?"

"Are you kidding? What'll I ask him, How are things in the rackets these days?"

"Listen, Mike, this is important stuff. I'll tell you the gory details later. You can figure out something to talk to him about."

He thought a minute. "Nelson's got so much he can't talk about, I lay you dough he won't even go near the microphone."

"He'll be flattered as hell. He's got a girl with him. He'll want to show off for her."

"I'll give it a whirl," Mike said. "Is that all there is to it?"

"No, I'll need your wife's help, too. Tell Buff to take Nelson's girl to the ladies' room. You know, the let's-powder-our-noses-while-the-men-talk routine. I need to talk to the girl alone and Danny can't know it. Listen, I wouldn't bull you about this thing. There's a lot at stake. You're an actor, pal. Pull it off. I know you can."

"I'll try, Maguire. I'll do my best."

"Thanks, Mike. I owe you one hell of a big favor."

"Forget it. Glad to help."

Then I called Forrester to report progress. "Not a hitch yet," I said.

"It's only begun. The hardest parts are yet to come."

"Relax, Wally. The worst that can happen is that we'll all get killed."

I beat it over to the Chez then. It was very crowded. I had only one danger and that was that George might show up to report in to Nelson. The ladies' room was close to the entrance. I waited there for Buff to bring the redhead out.

It took longer than I expected.

The redhead was surprised to see me. At first she was going to pretend not to know me, but Buff walked right up to me. "One thing about us," she said. "We always deliver."

"Thanks, Buff. You'll never know how much this means."

"There's a fire escape out there. Very cozy. Mike and I use it to get fresh air. I'll go powder my nose for as long as I think it's decent."

"If Nelson starts asking any questions about his girl, tell him she wasn't feeling too well and stretched out for a while in the little girl's room. O.K.?"

"Sure, Johnny." Then she turned to Marie. "Careful, dear. Nelson may be a gangster, but this one here is an Irishman."

I took Marie's hand and we went out on the fire escape.

We wasted a lot of time kissing before we got around to saying anything. She said, "I was so afraid you just forgot or couldn't do anything, Johnny. I can't put Danny off much longer."

"It's all arranged, baby. We're not alone. We've got the FBI helping us."

"The FBI?"

"Ever hear of them? Pretty fair outfit."

"What about Dad? I mean if the FBI is mixed up in this, will we be able to keep the thing about Dad a secret?"

"All arranged. Don't worry."

"What do I have to do?"

"This isn't going to be easy. Timing is the most important thing. I'm counting on one thing, baby. I know how anxious Danny is to get you in the sack. You've got to play coy, want the thing with all the trimmings. Get him to take you back to his place right away. Go upstairs and go in with him. Then by hook or crook get to the back door and unlock it."

"What if someone else is there? Those men of his may be around."

"He'll get rid of them if you tell him to. He'll want privacy. Tell him people in the apartment will make you nervous."

"Then what?"

"I'll be at the back door. If the coast is clear, I'll go right up to your room. If it isn't, I'll wait in the back hall until you can get Danny somewhere where he won't be able to see me come in."

"Johnny, do you think I'll be able to push Danny around like that, make him do everything I want?"

"You don't know much about sex, baby, do you? Until he finally gets you in your room, you'll be able to lead him by the nose."

"What's going to happen then?"

"You don't have to do anything until he comes to your room and he's ready. Then you're going to ask him for a shot."

"Of what?"

"Dope."

"But Johnny, I—"

"This is going to be the hard part, Red. Tell him you're no good without dope. Tell him it does something for you. Make it sound like this isn't going to be any fun unless you get a shot in the arm. You may have to go all the way through with it. I don't know. It depends on how fast the FBI steps into the picture. It won't hurt. And one more thing, Red. The minute you feel the needle go into your arm, scream, 'Now' as loud as you possiblycan."

"Is that the signal?"

"Yes. The FBI breaks the little scene up at that point. I hope."

"What if it doesn't work? What if he hasn't got any dope in the apartment?"

"He has. Don't worry about that. I've got a hunch he's got enough there to feed the whole country."

"But if something goes wrong, Johnny!"

"I'll be there, Red. Under the bed with my gun ready. Just don't worry."

"You're taking an awful chance for me, aren't you?"

"Don't forget, I'm the boy holding the seventy grand. I'm the boy Nelson has sworn to knock off. There's more to it than just you."

"That makes me feel a little better."

"But if I didn't have anything to do with it—if it was just you and I felt the way about you that I do—it wouldn't make any difference. I'd do it anyway."

She moved away from me, out of my arms. "Johnny, I can't go through with this."

"What are you talking about?"

"I can't go through with this. Not with you feeling the way you do."

"Talk straight, Red."

She faced me now. "This is so hard to say. I may be a terrible fool for telling you this, but I can't let you do this, not unless you know."

"Know what?" The bottom had dropped out of my stomach. Sweat broke out all over my body. I could feel it beading up under my clothes and the beads of perspiration fusing and running in rivulets down my back. "What is it I've got to know?"

"Before," she said. "In that shed. I said it was the first time and it wasn't. I lied. I think I lied deliberately because I wanted you to help me. There's another man. I met him in France. I'm so mixed up now, I don't know which is which. I don't know which is love and which isn't love."

"You mean you gave yourself to me just so I could help you out of this mess?"

"I'm not sure. I've been trying to decide myself. I don't think so, Johnny. I really don't. I wanted you. I loved you."

"You're talking in the past tense."

"I still love you. I still want you. But—"

"But what?"

"I'm not sure if I really love you or if it's only because I need you so much."

"When are you going to make up your mind?"

She was crying but I had had enough of tears. I'm a sucker for tears, but only up to a point. Then I stop. Then I get mad.

"It's so hard," she said, "to make up my mind now. I mean it's all so unsettled. Later, when I can look at things as they really are..."

"The hell with that. When you love someone you don't have to look at anything or figure anything out. Either it's there or it isn't there. Make up your mind."

"If you don't want to go ahead with this thing, I'll understand. I won't blame you under the circumstances."

"First you make a sucker out of me, now you want me to act like a heel."

"Johnny, it's not like you think. I didn't let you make love to me just because I needed your help. I swear that. I wanted you to make love to me. I would have died if you hadn't. It's just that—"

The fire-escape door opened. We froze. Buff's voice came through. "Your boyfriend is getting hard to handle."

"Go on back to Nelson, Red. You know the plans. Keep your head. Don't get frightened. Don't forget to yell the signal when that needle goes in. I'll be there to stop Nelson unless—unless you think he can help more than I can. Maybe you can work yourself up into wanting him, too. Maybe I'm not doing you a favor by breaking up this big love scene."

"Johnny, don't talk like that. Please."

"All right, get going. Do just as I said. It'll come out all right."

She came over to me, but I wasn't having any. "Get going," I said.

She touched my face with the tips of her fingers. Then wordlessly, she left me.

I held tight to the dirty iron railing of the fire escape. Below, there was a dirty city alley, overloaded with rubbish and debris. On either side, tall buildings hemmed me in. But when I looked up through the narrow slit between the two buildings, I saw the moon, full and bright, and there was the man in the moon smiling.

"Son of a bitch," I said aloud. "You're a son of a bitch."

CHAPTER FOURTEEN

The minute that he heard my voice, Forrester detected something wrong.

"There's nothing wrong," I said. "It's going like clockwork. I'm a sucker, that's all. I'm the biggest damn fool that ever walked."

"The girl?"

"What else makes a sap out of a guy?"

"Sorry, Johnny."

"Don't be sorry, Wally. You're going to get Danny Nelson tonight. You're going to get a raise. You're going to be queen of the May. What the hell have you got to be sorry about?"

"Take it easy, fellow. I've just been sitting here minding my own business."

"All right, Wally. Don't pay any attention to me. Get the wheels going. We're closing in for the kill."

I got to the apartment before Nelson and Marie did. Someone had relocked the back door but had neglected the windows. I opened one and climbed in. I got into the elevator and went right up to Danny's apartment and waited with my ear to his back door.

It took a long time. Maybe not as long as it seemed to me. I heard the lock being opened and waited. She didn't open the door. Then I heard her speak. "George! What are you doing here?"

"Me? I live here."

"I came down to get a glass of milk. Do you think there's any milk in the icebox?"

"Sure. I drink milk all the time. Danny keeps it for me."

I stood there motionless, leaning against the door, while the redhead and George drank milk. Then Danny came in. "Where you been, baby? I've been looking for you."

"I wanted a glass of milk," she said. "I ran into George here and we decided to drink together." I heard her force some laughter.

Then Danny said, "Any sign of that Maguire yet?"

"Not a thing, boss. I just spoke to Herman and Lefty. There ain't been a sign of him nowhere. They're going to keep looking, though."

"You get going, too, George. You're not going to find him by sitting here drinking milk. You heard what I said, didn't you? Get moving. I gave him until tonight. That guy's been smart long enough. Now, get him. Get out and get him. I want that dough. Are you going to let a punk like that outsmart you?"

"But Danny, you know I—"

"I don't know nothing but that I want Maguire and the dough. Tonight. You got that through your dumb head? Have you?"

"O.K., Danny, O.K."

When they were alone, Danny said, "Come on, I've been waiting for you."

Her voice was sweet as honey, the way it had been in the little shed. Turn it on and turn it off, I was thinking. "You go on and get ready, Danny," she said.

He laughed. "Me, I'm always ready. Whatever I need I got with me."

"But I always thought a famous man like you would have beautiful silk dressing gowns, fancy pajamas. I've always wanted something like this, a penthouse, beautiful clothes, a beautiful room." She hesitated. "And a man like you, Danny."

"You want it fancy, huh? I bet that's the way those guys in Hollywood do it, with all the trimmings. Silk pajamas, fancy bathrobes, stinking of perfume like a woman. Is that what you want, baby?"

"Something like that."

"You think I haven't got those things? You're wrong. You go up and wait for me. I'll show you. No matter what any of those Hollywood guys have got, Danny has got more and better. You go wait in your room for me. You'll see."

"You go ahead first, Danny. I want to finish my milk. Then I'll go up. Knock first. I want to be sure that I look lovely enough for you."

Nelson's voice had become low and husky. "You want to know something, kid? I don't need none of this fancy build-up business. I'm ready, like I am and right here."

"For me, Danny. Will you? Because I like the trimmings?"

"O.K., kid. This time I'll make it nice and fancy for you."

When he was gone, she opened the door. We didn't say a word. We walked into the living room and I unlocked the front door, leaving it open a crack. Then, together, we ran upstairs. Marie kept looking at me and there was pleading in her eyes. I pretended to pay no attention.

It was a tight fit, me under a bed. I thought of all the tight spots I had been in. This was the first time I had ever had to hide under a bed. Marie fooled around in the bedroom and I caught a glimpse of her as she came out, flowing in one of Gloria's fancy nightgowns.

I pulled my gun out, keeping it ready. I realized I should have taken my coat off because it was hotter than hell under that bed. But it was too late. I couldn't risk getting out there long enough to take it off.

Danny came back and all I saw of him were his ankles and feet. That was enough. He was wearing yellow silk pajamas and black patent-leather slippers. "Look pretty good, don't I, kid?"

"You look just wonderful, Danny."

"Those Hollywood guys got nothing on me. Feel this robe, feel the material. A thing like this costs real dough."

"It's beautiful, Danny."

"Hey, that nightgown fits you real good, honey. It makes you look like a million bucks. Come here."

I would have given anything if I could have been out of there. I hoped I could stick it out without losing control and letting Danny have it. I started counting silently. This kiss lasted a long time. "Hey," Danny said, "that's good. You got enthusiasm. Let me have some more." The second kiss lasted even longer. Then I saw Nelson's robe fall to the floor and he kicked off his slippers.

"Wait a minute, Danny," she said. "I'd like something first. I'd like a shot."

There was a pause. "You're kidding."

"No, I'm not, Danny. Really I'm not."

"A nice, clean kid like you?"

"You don't know what I'm like when I've had it. It does something to me. It lifts me way up and I kind of go crazy."

This girl was sensational. It was as if she had a script in front of her.

"You're sure you want this, kid?"

"Oh, Danny, please. You won't be sorry, I promise you."

"Come here," he said.

"No, Danny. After I get the shot."

"You got to coax me a little. You know how to coax me, don't you, baby?"

They were wrestling around right near the bed. "No, Danny, I've got to have the shot first. Honest." I heard the sound of cloth tearing and the ripped nightgown floated to the floor and fell beside Nelson's robe. My blood was up and my gun was ready. Hold it, Maguire. Hold it, Maguire. I had warned her it might be rough. I couldn't jump the gun now, not when we were so close to having Nelson where we wanted him.

I hoped that everything had gone smoothly with Forrester's men. If it had, they would be outside the bedroom door at that minute, waiting as I was waiting. But were they feeling inside what I was? This was a job to them. This girl was a trap, a decoy to them. It couldn't be hurting them. They hadn't loved her.

Then Nelson's gruff voice said, "That's what I mean, baby. Coax me."

She was almost crying. "Get it for me, Danny. Get it for me."

As he walked away from the bed to the far end of the room, I could see him. There was a complete wall of built-in wardrobes filled with Gloria's clothes. In the center there was a dressing table. The walls behind it and around it were all mirror. I saw Nelson reach under the dressing table, and he must have pressed a button because the whole dressing-table section swung out. There was a passage behind it. There's where he kept it. The dope was there and the money must have been there too. That's how Gloria Kirby knew where he hid it.

Nelson came out holding the needle. "You lie down on the bed, honey."

I felt the weight of her as she lay on the bed.

"You ready?" he asked.

"Yes, Danny." Her voice trembled. I held my breath and waited. Then it came, the signal shriek out of her throat in a terrified scream. "Now! Now!"

I waited for the men to burst in through the door.

Nothing happened.

"Now! Now!" She screamed it again and kept screaming it.

Nelson slapped her across the face.

From below there came a loud warning. "Danny, look out!" It was George's voice.

Then there was a shot. George's voice stopped.

Nelson moved fast. In one quick gesture he had the redhead off the bed and was holding her in front of him, using her as a shield. Forrester and his men burst in. Too late. I had to look at it, the wonderful, beautiful body pinned against Nelson, an armor of naked flesh no man would shoot through. The hypo needle dangled from her arm and there was blood around it.

There were two men with Forrester. All three men had their guns ready. But their guns were useless.

Wally said, "Let go of the girl, Nelson. We've got you now."

"You haven't got me. Go on, shoot, wise guys. Shoot through this pigeon."

"Let her go, Nelson."

"You got it wrong, boys. You're going to let me go." He shifted position, always keeping the girl in front of him. "Move away from that there door." Nothing happened. "Go ahead, move away. Did you ever watch while a woman's arm was broken? All I got to do is twist hard. She's got it coming. You want to see me do it or are you going to move away?" The other men looked at Forrester. He motioned with his head and they began moving away. "That's right," Danny said. "You wouldn't want to see nothing happen to this girl. Keep moving."

Carefully I aimed my gun. It was a dangerous shot. The bullet would go through Nelson and probably hit her. If he had been taller than she, I could have aimed at his head. This way I concentrated on winging him in the shoulder. He was a moving target and I couldn't be careless. I squeezed slowly.

It hit him in the shoulder and the impact of the shot thrust him forward and he hit a table. But it wasn't enough. He straightened up quickly, his face twisted with pain. He hadn't seen me, he didn't know my position. He took the dangling needle from the girl's arm and held the point in front of her face. "Wise guys," he mumbled. "Wise guys. Once more and I'll make this face look like raw meat. Once more."

Marie had been silent up until then, her eyes like two pieces of glass. She was bewildered, dazed, not realizing what was happening. But with that needle dangerously near her eye, she screamed. "Johnny, don't let him! Don't let him, Johnny!"

I fired again right at the base of his spine. It hit and he let go of the girl and she fell to the floor. I fired again and Danny fell, all blood and yellow silk pajamas.

I ran over to the girl. She was hit. The bullet had gone through Nelson and was lodged in her back.

Forrester said behind me, "Nelson is dead."

"The girl's been hit. Gall an ambulance."

One of Wally's men went to the phone, and Wally said, "I'm sorry, Johnny. I told you it was risky. It depended on too many things."

"Don't complain, Wally. You got Nelson. Behind that closet in there is all the evidence you need against him and all his men."

"I'm not even thinking about that. I'm thinking about the girl. We ran into trouble. One of Nelson's men. Otherwise we would have been here on time."

The redhead was unconscious. The needle was on the floor. I picked it up. "This is the way to get rich, Wally." I looked over at the dead Nelson. "Rich and rotten."

I heard the sirens coming down the street. I was in a fog. Confusion buzzed all around me. Wally was telephoning and there were people running in and out. I stayed on the floor beside her until an intern lifted me away. I watched as he examined her.

"Well?" I asked.

"I don't know," he said. "Maybe." Then to the orderlies, "Let's make it snappy, boys."

CHAPTER FIFTEEN

In my time, I've watched people die.

I huddled over her as the ambulance sirened its way through the city streets. I couldn't tell whether she would live or not. She lay lifeless and immobile. The bullet from my gun was in her back. It was better this way, I thought, no matter what happened. Nelson hadn't been fooling. He would have mutilated her if I hadn't stopped him with my gun.

She regained consciousness suddenly and unexpectedly. Her eyes opened wide and her lips formed a smile. I was worried. This happens sometimes just before death. There is a sudden rush of strength, a last burst of life. I looked over at the intern. The expression on his face didn't change.

"Johnny," she whispered.

"Don't try to talk, Red. Save your strength. You're going to be all right."

"What happened, Johnny?" Her voice was scarcely audible.

"It's all right, Red. Nelson is dead. Everything is safe. Your brother is going to get off."

Her face screwed up with pain. She bit her lip until the wave of pain subsided. "Thank you."

"You've got nothing to thank me for. I did it for myself, too. I'm safe now, too."

"I'm glad, Johnny. I'm glad." Then her head fell to the side and her eyes closed.

"Doc," I yelled. "Look at her."

He held her wrist. "She's all right," he said. "We'll be at the hospital in a minute."

They tried to stop me from going into the hospital room, but I strong-armed my way past them. Forrester had followed the ambulance in his car. He flashed his card at the protesting authorities and they let me stay with her. My breathing was short and hard as the hospital doctor examined her.

"What do you say, doc?"

"I can't say for sure. She has a good chance."

Then just before they took her to the operating room, she came to again. "Call my father, Johnny. Tell him I'm all right and that Sandy is all right. Tell him everything will be all right from now on. And tell him to tell Paul."

"Paul?"

She closed her eyes for a moment. "He's the boy, Johnny."

I took her hand and squeezed it. "Yeah," I said, "he's the boy."

While she was in the operating room, I put through a long-distance call to Sanford Wharton II. "This is John Maguire," I said. "I'm calling about your daughter."

"Where is she? We've been looking for her everywhere. She disappeared."

I told him the story, leaving out the gruesome parts of it. I told him he didn't have to worry about Nelson any more, none of his family did. I had to tell him Marie was in the hospital. "But she's going to be all right." I said. "It's just a little more than a scratch."

"I'm flying there right away," he said.

"O.K. She'll be glad to see you. And she asked me to tell you to contact Paul."

"Paul is there. In Chicago. He's nearly crazy looking for her. Call him and tell him. He's been to the police and everything." He told me where Paul was staying and I phoned the hotel. Paul must have been sitting on top of the telephone waiting for word about Marie. I gave him the story and he started for the hospital.

When I came out of the phone booth, Wally Forrester was standing by the door to the operating room waiting for me. "Any word, Wally?"

"No, not yet. Don't worry, Johnny, she'll be all right."

"It's *my* bullet in her back."

"You did the smartest thing, Johnny."

"It's easy to say. It's hard to believe."

"Listen, Johnny. I'd like to stay with you but there are a thousand things to do to clean up after this."

"Go ahead, Wally. I'll get the missing seventy thousand dollars to you tomorrow."

"From the bank robbery? You've got it?"

I nodded. "Don't ask questions. And remember what you promised about that kid in jail."

"I'll get him off, Johnny."

"There was a girl named Gloria Kirby, a friend of Danny's."

"I've heard of her."

"She's dead," I said. "She's an unidentified stiff in the city morgue. She had a vault somewhere with a confession in it, facts and figures that are powerful enough to put a finger on a lot of the boys you've been trying to nail."

"This has turned out to be quite a thing, Johnny. I'm grateful to you. You know what my stock is going to be worth in the Bureau after this." He smiled. "I even forgive you for Clarice Lovelace."

"One more thing. The girl in the movie house—you can pull your man off but leave her there. I want to tell her about this myself."

"O.K., Johnny. Good luck."

The waiting was interminable. There were doctors and nurses rushing back and forth into the operating room. No one knew or would tell me anything about the redhead.

Then Paul came. He was the same type as Sanford Wharton III, except that he was older and stockier. Breeding was embroidered all over him. I thought, This was the man for her; this is the kind of man who was made for her. She had no business with a punchy lug from the wrong side of the tracks. I was out of her league. And there was something else. I knew it then. I was out of her league and I didn't want in.

When the doctor came out of the operating room, Paul went right up to him. "I'm Miss Wharton's fiancé," he said. "How is she?"

"She's going to be fine," he said. "Just fine."

They talked some more but I had heard enough. She was going to be all right. That's all I wanted to know.

There was a clock near the cashier's window at the Clark Theatre. It was three o'clock in the morning. I bought a ticket and walked in.

The theatre was almost empty. Tina was sitting alone, near the back. I sat down beside her. Slowly, cautiously, she turned her head. When she saw it was I, tears filled her eyes. "Johnny..."

"It's O.K.," I whispered. "Everything is O.K."

"Everything?"

I nodded. "Yeah, everything."

"Johnny, I want to tell you that—"

"Shh. The movie is going on. Let's watch it."

"I've seen it a thousand times."

"Any good?"

"Oh, Johnny," she sighed.

I settled back in the seat. It was a cowboy movie, all right. Lots of horses and lots of shooting. In a little while I took Tina's hand and held it. A small, hard object was in her hand and it fell into mine.

The key.

THE END

Made in the USA
Middletown, DE
04 November 2021